BLOOD SHOT

"Don't touch your iron or you're dead men," Rebecca Caldwell barked, fisting a matched pair of Smith & Wesson .44's aimed at the outlaws.

"Well, missy, ain't you a sight," said a third man from behind, pointing a side-by-side Greener at her back. "Now, why don't you just—"

She turned her head slightly, then snapped two quick shots at the fat jasper holding the scatter gun. One round took him in the side of the head and drove him back into the car. The shotgun fell to the floor and discharged, showering double-aught buck clean through the roof.

WHITE SQUAW BY E. J. HUNTER

WHITE SQUAW #14   (2075, $2.50)
As Rebecca Caldwell and her trusted companion Lone
Wolf are riding back to the Dakota Territory, their train is
ambushed by angry Sioux warriors. Becky ultimately finds
out that evil Grover Ridgeway is laying claim to the land
that the Indians call their own—and decides to take Grover
in hand and pump out some information. Once she has
him firmly in line, the White Squaw blows the cover off of
his operation!

WHITE SQUAW #18   (2585, $2.95)
Hot on the heels of her long-time enemy, Roger Styles, Rebecca Caldwell is determined to whip him into shape once
and for all. Headed for San Antonio and eager for action,
Becky's more than ready to bring the lowdown thieving
Styles under thumb—especially when she discovers he's
made off with her gold. Luck seems to be on the White
Squaw's side when Styles falls into her lap—and ends up
behind bars.

WHITE SQUAW #19   (2769, $2.95)
Rebecca Caldwell was in no mood for romance after
owlhoots murdered her lover Bob Russel. But with the
rich, handsome teamster, Win Harper, standing firm and
coming on hard, Becky feels that old familiar fire rising up
once more . . . and soon the red-hot halfbreed's back in
the saddle again!

*Available wherever paperbacks are sold, or order direct from the
Publisher. Send cover price plus 50¢ per copy for mailing and
handling to Zebra Books, Dept. 3376, 475 Park Avenue South,
New York, N.Y. 10016. Residents of New York, New Jersey and
Pennsylvania must include sales tax. DO NOT SEND CASH.*

#22

DESERT CLIMAX

E.J. HUNTER

ZEBRA BOOKS
KENSINGTON PUBLISHING CORP.

ZEBRA BOOKS

are published by

Kensington Publishing Corp.
475 Park Avenue South
New York, NY 10016

First printing: April, 1991

Printed in the United States of America

CHAPTER 1

The teamster in his mid twenties pushed the brown Stetson back on his head and laughed, a mean, dirty laugh that made the Mexican boy in front of him cringe in the fragile light of dusk. It would be fully dark in another five minutes.

"What's the matter, greaser, think you're as good as a white man? Think you can walk on the board-walk like a real man?" His fist shot out and hit the surprised Mexican on the chin, driving him back against a heavy adobe wall. Three more punishing blows hit his mouth and nose so quickly that the Mexican couldn't defend himself.

Blood gushed from Pedro's nose. He brought up his hands to defend himself, and the teamster in the red shirt laughed again.

"Damn, thinks he's a pugilist now, ain't that disgusting? A damn greaser Mex thinks he can fight."

The short Mexican youth slashed out a fist and at the same time kicked at the anglo. His fist only grazed the teamster's face as the man ducked, but the youth's shoe slammed into his attacker's crotch. The shoe leather drove up between the man's legs, catching the heavy scrotum, jamming it higher until the leather crushed one testicle against the sturdy pelvic bones. The kick brought a scream of agony from the

5

teamster and dumped him onto the boardwalk. He lay writhing in agony in the Taos, New Mexico, dirt and sand which the wind had blown onto the heavy planks.

"Bastard!" the teamster choked out, then curled into a protective ball, pulling his knees up to his chest to try to relieve the pain of the crushed testicle. His whimpering soon gushed into braying screams of pain.

The other two white men who had been enjoying the Mex-baiting show growled and leaped forward. One punch from a large man's huge fist dropped the youth to the boardwalk. The other teamster kicked the downed Mexican in the ribs. The dusk deepened, and soon it was hard to see fifty feet along the street.

Only after the boot slammed into his side did Pedro make any sound. He choked back a scream as two ribs broke. He stared at the tall anglos with eyes of fear. He figured he was going to die. It wouldn't be the first time in Taos the anglos had beaten a Mexican to death.

The Mexicans had been in the town much longer than the newcomer white men, but it didn't seem to matter. Now there were twice as many whites as the brown-skinned Mexicans in the centuries-old trade village of Taos.

Pedro scooted backward, sliding along the side of the building by pushing with his feet and scrabbling along on his hands and his rear end.

"Where you going you crotch-kicking greaser bastard?" the heavily muscled teamster asked. "Think you can get away with putting our friend down? Didn't think about us being here, did you, you shit-faced little greaser?"

He kicked again, but this time, Pedro surged away from the angry boot, the movement punishing his ribs and making him gasp from the continuing pain in his side.

"He hit me first," Pedro said, starting to stand up

6

against the building.

From the other side, the third man jumped in and drove his heavy fist into the side of Pedro's cheek, breaking the cheek bone and smashing him back down to the dirty surface of the boardwalk.

"Got to kill the little son-of-a-bitch," the muscled teamster said.

"Hell yes. He hurt old Percy bad back there. Dark enough now nobody gonna see us. We can stomp the bastard to death in about two minutes."

"Yeah, and then get Percy to a doctor. Damn, he must of got smashed up good. He ain't moved since he went down."

"Me first," the muscled teamster growled. He stepped up to the downed Mexican youth and pulled his heavy boot backward.

From less than twenty feet away, a handgun belched fire, and a hot .45 slug tore into the muscled man's shoulder, driving him back a step. He stumbled over his own feet and went down in a disjointed pile of arms and legs near the wall.

"What the hell?" the second teamster still standing cried as he dug for the six-gun in well-worn leather at his right thigh.

"No, señor. Leave the *pistola* in the pouch if you wish to live."

The decidedly thick Mexican accented voice stopped the young teamster from grabbing for iron.

"This is no business of yours," the undamaged teamster in his red shirt said, his hand on the gun but making no move to draw it.

"You are wrong, young anglo, you are decidedly mistaken. It is my business. All of my people are my business. You may have heard of me. I am Antonio Sinfuegos."

"Yeah, and I'm the king of England. Never heard of you."

The shadowed figure came closer, and now the teamsters could see him. He was only an inch over

7

five feet tall, slender, and dressed in the traditional Mexican fashion of a rich man. His wide-brimmed sombrero had a hundred dollars' worth of silver on it, and his short jacket was decorated with more silver and some blue-green stones. His shirt was starkly white in the darkness.

The revolver he held was aimed directly between the two teamsters.

"Perhaps you know my other name. Some people call me *el Zopilote*."

The man on the ground groaned as he held his bleeding shoulder. "The Buzzard? Damn. Yeah, everybody this end of the country knows about you. Look, about the kid. We're sorry. We didn't mean to hurt the boy, just having some fun with him. You can understand that. He's in good shape, just be a little sore."

"Of course. Three anglos beating up on one sixteen-year-old Mexican. Just entertainment, a game for some drunken anglo mule skinners. What could be more understandable." The words came dripping with sarcasm and anger.

"You white men are worse than the Pueblo Indians. You come bursting in here with your wagons and your cheap trade goods and force my people out of their homes and stores. I am Mexican. True, I am a *bandido*, but I live by a code much higher than yours. I do not torture and kill harmless boys. But the men who do this kind of violence to one of my people are another matter."

He shot the younger man where he stood against the building. The round bored straight through his heart, and he died writing on the boardwalk. The teamster with the wounded shoulder tried to crawl away, but the second round from the revolver slammed into the back of his head and blew his forehead against the dull brown of the unpainted adobe wall.

El Zopilote turned toward the man who had been

crotch kicked. Percy had risen to his knees, his dark eyes wild with fear and panic. He lifted no farther. The bandit's third bullet tore through his crotch, slicing through his privates and dumping the man against the adobe wall.

For a moment the bandit listened as the man screamed in terror and agony, then *el Zopilote* put a round through the screaming teamster's heart. *El Zopilote* holstered his weapon and hurried to the Mexican youth, Pedro, helped him to stand and led him away down the dark street.

The bandit chief gave him a ten-dollar gold piece and walked him to a Mexican healer who looked at the wounds, scowled and swore softly in Spanish as he bound up the young man's chest with a white bandage to help hold the ribs in place. Nothing had punctured the lung. Pedro would be good as new in a month or two.

El Zopilote stood outside the small shack of discarded boards and pieces of roofing tin where Pedro lived. The *bandido* tightened one hand into a fist and shook it in front of him. The damn anglos were at it again. Would he have to kill every one of them before they learned to treat Mexicans as human beings?

It might just come to that. He might have to bring together all of his men and capture the whole town of Taos and make it his headquarters. He pondered the thought as he moved off in the darkness.

Webb Bryce had been a surveyor before he went into contracting. Now he sighted through his own transit, to align the front of the building precisely right and exactly in line with another building a block down along the main dirt street of Taos. Some day this avenue would be paved and have concrete sidewalks just like San Francisco. He wanted to be sure nobody had to tear down his building because it was out of alignment with the others.

He waved both hands to his sides after having moved several times the man's hand who was positioning the plumb bob down the way. The man dropped the bronze-pointed device to mark exactly where the structure's corner should be. They used flat rocks as pier blocks to give the building a firm foundation.

It was to be a warehouse for the Inter-Mountain Freight Lines, which now brought in tons of goods up the trail from the Atchison, Topeka and Santa Fe station. There was no railroad to Taos, and might never be, Webb considered.

The little town sat in the midst of the Sangre de Cristo Mountains, fifty-five tough trail miles north of Santa Fe. It was high country with Wheeler Peak towering over the town at 13,161 feet due north. Taos was hot in the summer and had deep snow in the winter. He'd have to push hard to get this building put up before the snow came.

He'd planned the warehouse to be eighty feet wide and one hundred feet long, making it the largest building in town. It would be of wood construction, though most of the town was still adobe block. It was a fine building material, huge bricks in effect made from adobe clay, pounded into a form ten inches wide, fourteen inches long and four inches deep and allowed to bake brick-hard in the Taos sun.

Only he didn't have time to make that many adobe bricks. Besides, he ran the local lumberyard, such as it was, and he got the lumber at wholesale prices.

Webb had done all right the three years he had been in town. He was now on the city council and a deacon in the Baptist church. Everything was going fine.

He frowned as one of his Mexican workmen stumbled and knocked down a form that he was lifting. The form broke as it fell, so he'd have to have it rebuilt.

"Damn Mex!" a white carpenter growled as he went past Webb. "Wish they'd stay down below

10

the border."

Webb could feel the tension, but he used both Mexican and white workers and an occasional Pueblo Indian who wanted to learn the ways of the white man. Most of the time his crew got along fine.

They got the foundation rocks all set that day and the beams in place for the base of the structure. Then they began to set in the joists for the floor. Production was moving along well. He took one final look at it when the men quit work at six o'clock. Yes, the structure was solid and in good shape.

The next morning Webb Bryce walked two blocks down Main Street to breakfast. He went by the warehouse site just to check. When he could see the spot, he stared in disbelief at the building. It wasn't there. The corner where he had worked yesterday was again in its native condition. The eighteen pier-block rocks he had hauled in had vanished. The beams they had set in place with precision using his transit were gone. None of the one-by-ten floor joists was there either. It was as if they had worked the day before and done absolutely nothing. Even the shallow holes they had dug on one end of the sloping lot to set the pier blocks in on the level had been filled in and smoothed over.

The lot looked as if no white man had touched it in a hundred years.

What happened to the stones and the beams? He searched and tried to find materials. In the dirt street he found tracks, drag marks of travois and horses. He followed one set that angled to the north, and he found the pier blocks five hundred yards away at the edge of town. All eighteen of them were there in a string along the side of the road where they had been dumped.

The heavy beams had been dragged the other way but had not been cut up or damaged. He found the twelve-foot joists to the west where they had been tumbled down a gully.

Webb Bryce shook his head in anger and disbelief. Who was playing this kind of a joke on him? It had to be a joke. One of his friends in town, maybe. But someone had gone to a lot of work. The mean trick had cost him a day's wages for the crew, but little else. He could stand it.

He continued on to the Taos Cafe and had ham and eggs, two cups of coffee and a stack of hotcakes. It would be a hard day again. He'd have to start all over again. First he had to go home and get his transit.

When he got to the job site just before seven, he stopped and stared in amazement. An hour before there had been only a barren lot next to several tumbled-down, ancient adobe structures that the early Indians must have lived in.

The complex of adobe-made buildings covered half a block. It was a "village" of sorts, a meandering assembly of adobe-built rooms that looked as if they had been added haphazardly, as if one was built when it was needed for a new family member or a new family. Most were only one story high, but in places there were two-story sections and even some with three stories.

Now, instead of a bare building lot beside the sprawling, run-down Indian houses, the area had been turned into a ceremonial ground by more than a hundred Indians. The Tewa Pueblos had come in their full formal attire. Every warrior wore a head-dress with eagle feathers. The women had on white, beaded dresses of bleached doeskin and fancy beaded headbands.

A small fire had been built, and the Indian men sat around it cross-legged and grim. Webb decided it looked like what he had heard about Indian council fires!

Two Feathers, the medicine man and ceremonial leader of the Tewa Pueblos, danced slowly around the council fire. He chanted too softly for Webb to hear the words, which were most likely in the

12

Indian lingo.

By now Taos was awake, and half a hundred people had crowded around the edge of the Indian gathering to watch the ceremony. Few of the whites or Mexicans had seen anything like this from the usually calm and peaceful Pueblo tribes.

Now the slow rhythm of drums came, and Webb moved so that he could see the council better. The drummers picked up the beat, and the ceremonial leader stepped aside as six young men came to the fire and danced around it. They wore only their breechclouts and strange and wild masks.

With a sudden flurry of fast dancing, the drum stopped, and the dancers twirled to a controlled stop at the same moment.

Gray Squirrel, the leader of the Taos band of the Tewa Pueblos, stood and stared long at the fire. He intoned some incantations, then turned to the council and spoke briefly in his native language.

Shorty Dunston edged up to Webb and tugged at his sleeve.

"I know some of that palaver out there, Bryce. Seeing how they leveled the start of your construction project, I figured you'd want to know what was going on. Only cost you three beers after this is over. You want to know what the chief is saying?"

"Damn right! I had a building started here yesterday. Invested a lot of money and time in it. Now looks like the damn Injuns tore it down and hauled it off. What the hell is happening here?"

Shorty grinned, nodded and then listened to the words the headman was saying. He snorted. "By damn, it's the ritual of the dead. I lived with the Tewas for a time. Had me a little squaw out there; but the pox got her, so I come back to town, oh, maybe twenty years ago. Learned to palaver with them red men right good.

"I knew when them *kachina* dancers came out with their masks on that it was gonna be a damned

13

big ceremony. Lordy, lordy, it certainly is!"

Bryce scowled at the short, balding man who only had one eye. The black patch that usually covered the healed-over hollow where his left eye had been gouged out in a barroom brawl was not in place this morning.

"Ritual of the dead? What the hell's that? Why don't they go to their damn burial ground for that?"

Shorty chuckled. "Makes sense, Bryce. That's what they did. This is one of the most sacred burial grounds of half a dozen Pueblo tribes around here. They call it the chief of chiefs' sacred burial place."

"Can't be. Maxwell Montrose owns that plot of land. I checked with the county clerk. It's registered all legal and proper. What he don't own is all that old wreck of hovels over there, the old pueblo."

"Seems to me you got one passel of trouble, Bryce. The headman there is saying that this is the chief of chiefs' burial grounds, and it's sacred even if it is surrounded by white men and Mexicans. He's saying that there isn't a chance in a rattler's tail that anybody is going to desecrate that land and cover up the graves.

"Doing that would cause any of the old chiefs who didn't make a quick leave-taking of their bones to be trapped. See, if a building went up there, the spirits couldn't get away from the bones, because spirits can't get free, 'cause they can't go through wood or adobe."

Shorty looked up at the over-six-foot-tall Bryce. "I'd say you got some mighty big troubles. Bound to be some Indians camping out on the edge of this sacred ground, or maybe in the pueblo ruins that they still have right there close by. You try to get back to work on that land without some approval from them, could mean we'd have an Indian war right here in Taos.

"These Tewas hold great respect for the dead. You got to remember that these tribes and their ancestors

14

been living here in Taos way back into the beginning of time. The old shaman out at the pueblo used to tell me stories about the Tewas being in this valley for more than ten thousand years.

"I know blamed well that the Spanish stopped by here in 1540 and again in 1598. Hell, us whites and the Mexes too are the interlopers. The Injuns know for sure they been here for three hundred years. They can prove that with their picture scrolls of deer hide."

"Damn!" Bryce said. "The city council better get into this. Think I'll call a meeting. I sure as hell can't build a warehouse today."

He went around the crowd finding his workmen and told them to locate the others and pass the word that they'd have to take the day off. At least today.

He found Shorty again and took him along as he called together the four other men who made up the Taos city council. He wanted Shorty to tell them about the burial ground and how the Indians felt.

The five-man Taos city council consisted of four merchants and a rancher who lived in town but ran a big spread a few miles out. Usually the council figured what was good for business was also good for the little town of Taos. Everyone was there but the rancher. The four men stared at each other for a minute after Shorty finished telling them about the burial site of the chief of chiefs'.

"Looks like we got ourselves one hell of a big problem here," Josh Randall said. Josh owned the hotel, a saloon and two small stores. "We can't just run the savages out of there. Damn, a sacred-ground burial site. That's the one item that would get the Pueblos stirred up and mad enough to fight. We got to come up with something damn good, and damn soon."

CHAPTER 2

Macario and Felipe sat on their horses five miles north of Taos. They waited for Carmelo, who soon rode up on his prancing black mare.

Macario was no more than twenty-five, had short dark hair, a black moustache and snapping, hooded eyes. The other two were a little younger.

"Now we do it," he said. "We can sell them for thirty dollars each after a two-day drive. We'll have enough money to take it easy for half a year."

Felipe shook his head. He was shorter than the other two, and his horse, a fifteen-year-old mare, showed the wear of the climb. He wore a Montana peak hat and scowled.

"One thing I learned is that when something seems too easy, there must be a good reason. You say there ain't any guards around the horses. Maybe that's only what you want to think. Maybe you didn't take a long enough look. If I was guarding a hundred prime trading horses, I wouldn't leave them alone in some mountain meadow without at least a few guards."

"All talk, Felipe. You said you wanted to come along. You come now or turn around. This is the place. We need you, but hell, I guess splitting the money two ways will make up for the extra work

Carmelo and I'll have. What will you do?''

Carmelo only grinned. It was all Carmelo ever did. Nobody knew if he could talk or not because no one had ever heard him speak. He was a head taller than both the others, and some said he had some *gringo* blood, but again nobody knew for sure.

"Damn, let's do it," Felipe said at last. "Let's go get those horses.''

"Yeah!" Macario shouted, and they turned and rode down a small pass that opened into a mile-long meadow high in the Sangre de Cristo Mountains north of Taos. For months now, the Taos Pueblo Indians had been pasturing their trading stock there. This year the big trading fair would come the first week in September again as it had for centuries.

Macario had no idea how the Indians from all over the Southwest and the southern plains knew when September 1 came, but they arrived within a few days of the date every year. Many sought horses.

Macario had heard that the Pueblo Indians had been the main source of horses when the animals were first introduced to the plains tribes. Back in 1680 the Pueblo Indians' revolt against the Spanish had resulted in the abandonment of several thousand Spanish horses in the area. The Pueblos quickly saw their value and captured the animals and began trading them to the plains tribes for goods the Pueblos needed.

The Pueblos were going to be short of trading stock this year for the big fair, Macario decided.

They rode for two miles down the faint deer trail toward the valley and the small stream there. Deer and elk used the path to go down for water.

Ten minutes later, they saw the horses. Most of them were grouped at this end of the valley.

"Must be almost two hundred there!" Macario gloated. "Wish we had ten men and we'd take them all.''

17

"How many can the three of us handle?" Felipe asked.

"We'll try for thirty. That will be at least nine hundred dollars, three hundred each! We can live for two years on that much *dinero!*"

They moved closer now, as silently as they could. For a half hour they sat just inside the rim of brush and trees watching the valley and especially the trees around the edge. They could find no guards, no small cooking fires, no sign of any Indians at all.

Macario nodded. "Let's go get them. Let's do it the slow, safe way. We'll tie rope halters on them as we come up to them. No hard riding, no panic. We snub down the halters and trail them on a lead line behind our own mounts.

"When we each have a string of ten behind us, we ride out the far side of the valley and head for that notch in the hill. It's a pass down into Green Valley. We ride back south two miles, then trail over the next two valleys to the Bar-B Ranch and our new-found fortune. Let's go."

They rode out from the trees, walking their mounts casually. The first few horses they came to shied away, then went on grazing. When the three young rustlers were a quarter of the way into the herd, Macario nodded, and they parted and began to ease up along the horses and slip a noose over each animal's neck. Then quickly they made a loop for a bridle and tied the mount to a lead line behind their own horses.

They each had one animal in tow when a horse began moving toward them. It seemed to carry no rider, only an Indian war bridle with a loop of rope around the animal's lower jaw, and a tight, wide strap of leather around the horse's back and chest.

Without warning, an Indian lifted up from the far side of the war pony and raised a rifle. He shouted something in English, but the three Mexican youths

18

did not understand the *gringo* tongue. Then he said something in his native language. Before he got it out, Macario pulled his six-gun. The rifle the warrior carried spat once, the booming sound ringing through the meadow.

He had fired at Macario, but missed. The round slammed past him and hit Felipe in the chest as he rode forward. Felipe jolted backward, lost his seat on the saddle and flipped to the ground where he lay without moving.

As soon as he'd seen the Indian's rifle, Macario had drawn his six-gun, an old Army Colt .45. He fired twice at the Indian, who was trying to get another round in his rifle. Then Macario kicked his horse in the sides and fled, angling toward the pass they had used to ride into the valley.

Carmelo sat on his horse a moment, not fully understanding what had happened. He saw Felipe fall, then saw Macario fire at the Indian. When Macario turned and fled, Carmelo did the same. He cut loose the horse he had captured, and caught up with his friend just as the rifle boomed twice behind them. Neither round hit the pair as they crashed into the brush and trees and out of sight of the guard with the horses.

They paused, and Macario looked back.

"*Madre de Dios!* I didn't think they had any guards. They sneaked up on us. Not our fault. Damn, poor Felipe." He shook his head. "Too bad, but when he came with us, he knew the risks; he was just unlucky."

On the way back to Taos, Macario formed a plan. Felipe would be missed. They would report what happened, almost. The Indians had killed Felipe. The sheriff should know about it. It was his county. A grin spread over Macario's face as he rode. He'd get even with those damn Tewa Indians!

Late that afternoon, Macario rode up to the

sheriff's office in Taos and tied his horse at the rail. Inside he held his hat in his hand and used his few words of English. Soon a deputy came who spoke Spanish. He told Macario that they only had an acting sheriff now because the elected sheriff quit and went to Oregon, but they would listen. Then Macario let the story pour out.

"My friend Felipe and I were riding in the mountains thinking about gold prospecting when six Tewa Indians rode us down and shot Felipe for no reason at all. They shot at me too; but I rode away as fast as I could, and they let me go. I demand that the Indians be punished. They shot down my friend."

Macario told the story twice again, and more people listened. The deputy translated what Macario said into English. They asked him to show on a map where they had been riding, and he pointed to an area near the place where the death had occurred.

He answered their questions. No, he couldn't identify any of the Indians. It had happened so quickly. Most of the Indian men looked alike to him anyway, he told the acting sheriff.

The *gringo* lawmen and the one Mexican deputy left him alone and talked among themselves. A half hour later they said that they had sent someone to notify Felipe's family and Macario was free to go.

At the door, the Spanish-speaking deputy caught up to Macario and stopped him.

"We'd like you to ride back up there tomorrow and show us where the body is so we can bring it back. If we find any Tewas along the way, we'll talk to them about the young man."

Macario said he could do that, then hurried out, eager now to get home. His father would be wondering about him. This idea to get rich hadn't worked. The next one would. He had lots of ideas.

*   *   *

20

Rebecca Caldwell and Marshall Aaron Hawkins had swung down from the Atchison, Topeka and Santa Fe mixed train at the last water stop and gone back to check on their horses in the stock car just in back of the second coach.

Rebecca's long summer recuperation in the arms of Aaron had ended in Flagstaff, Arizona, and now she was on her way to visit her stepson, Joey, in Texas. She hadn't spent enough time with him lately, and now was her chance. Starret and his whole operation were wiped out. Now she had time.

The direct train would have taken her south from Albuquerque, but she had turned north to visit an old and dear friend in Santa Fe. She, too, had been too long neglected. Now the train was less than half a day out of Santa Fe. As the cars rushed higher into the mountains, she relaxed. It would be a good visit. She looked back to her favorite mount.

Sila, her big Appaloosa with the spots on his rump, was making the trip fine. In his stall, he took a lump of sugar from her and looked for an apple, but she had run out.

"Look, you trickster, you be good and maybe soon we'll be able to take a run along the tracks."

Marshall Aaron Hawkins grinned at her. "You treat that animal like he was part of your family," the lawman from Flagstaff said. Rebecca and the marshall had come on this run to Santa Fe after spending most of the summer prosecuting the last of the Chris Starret outlaws in Flag. Starret had died in the rockfall, but numerous others of his band of killers had to be tried. Now all were convicted and hung.

"This Appaloosa trickster has helped me get out of more than one tight spot, and I appreciate him," Rebecca said. "How is that four-footed mongoose you brought along doing?"

The dun was not having a good trip. The mare had thrashed around in her stall for the last few miles and

21

had flecks of sweat on her. They wiped down the mare, and calmed her. A lump of sugar did as much as anything, and at last she settled down.

When they had gotten off the train at the last stop, they told the conductor that they would be in the stock car until the next stop. He had nodded. Many passengers who traveled with stock this way were protective of them. The road didn't feed or water them; that was the job of the stock owner.

With the two animals content, Rebecca and Aaron stood by the open boxcar door and watched the countryside roll by.

"Might as well sit and be comfortable," Aaron said, motioning to some freshly spread straw which would be used to replace the straw now in the stalls.

They sat on the straw, and his hand touched her shoulder. "Becky, it's been a wonderful summer. Too bad those trials didn't last a bit longer."

She bent and kissed him quickly, a sexy gleam in her deep blue eyes. When their lips parted, she grinned impishly. "Some of the best times were in that big feather bed of yours. I'll always remember that bed and you when I think of Flag."

He kissed her back, and as happened so often before, the rockets went off and their blood boiled; and she pushed him down on the hay and dropped on top of him.

"It's been a long time since I've had a literal roll in the hay, and I want one now," Rebecca said, her voice low and heavily toned with passion.

Her hips ground against his, and he could feel the raw heat of her body through both their clothes. Her mouth devoured him, kissing his eyes, his mouth, then down his cheeks. She pushed her tongue into his ear, and he moaned.

"Woman, you trying to get me excited?"

As an answer she movd to his belt, opened it and unbuttoned his fly, then spread back his pants. She pulled down his short underwear and laughed softly when his erect manhood sprang up, purple, engorged and ready to do battle.

Gently she stroked him with one hand, and used the other to massage his tender balls in their heavy sack.

"Now you're getting downright sexy," Aaron whispered. "Think I should close the door?"

She shook her head. "If we begin to stop, we can adjust our clothes in plenty of time. I don't want you to move!"

She bent and kissed the purple tip of him, then lathered him with her tongue down both sides of the long shaft. She moved back and unbuttoned the fasteners on her blouse and pulled it off, then lifted her chemise over her head.

Her fine breasts swung out, pink tipped with generous tinted areolas. She lowered one pointed morsel into his mouth. He sucked on it a moment; then she gave him the other one.

"Your turn first," she said softly. She went back to his crotch and took his lance in her mouth, sucking it in farther and farther until he gasped in surprise.

Then she closed her eyes and began to pump up and down on him. His hips picked up the motion and opposed it to thrust him deeper yet in her mouth and throat.

"Be careful, damn careful!" he whispered, but the passion colored his voice. His hips pumped upward harder, faster. She bobbed and bobbed. His breath came gasping in heavy lungfuls now as he tensed and his hips pounded upward, and her mouth took all of him.

"Oh, damn, you know I love it this way!" he shouted, then he stiffened again, every muscle in his body tightened as his hips spasmed upward and he shot his cream into her mouth.

She gulped and swallowed it all each time he jetted

into her. Six then eight times he thrust upward, lifting her head a foot higher, and then he fell back, spent, drained, exhausted beyond all reason.

She cleaned him off, then lay against him, covering him, protecting him, watching the door. She sensed that the train was still at speed.

Aaron died for a few minutes, then he roused and watched this marvelous woman.

"Beautiful!" he whispered.

"Yes, it was fine."

"No, I mean you. I love that wildness, that animal-like Sioux lusting that takes over your body now and then. You're so beautiful and sexy I can't believe it. That's why I couldn't stay in Flag and let you ride away from me."

She hushed him and bent and sucked on his man nipples; then she reached down and gently began bringing him back to hardness.

"My turn," she said. She had him ready again quickly, and they sat side by side in the straw. He bent and kissed her breasts, and she stroked him gently, then reached under her traveling skirt and pulled down her soft white bloomers. She lifted her skirt around her waist, dropped to her hands and knees and pushed her round, tight little bottom toward him.

"You know how I love it best," she said, her voice a low rumble distorted by her lust. Aaron grinned and went to his knees behind her. He moved forward and gently nudged her heartland. She wailed in delight. Then he probed ahead, found exactly the right place and thrust into her so quickly she gasped in surprise and wonder.

"Oh, damn!" she screeched. She looked over her shoulder at him and nodded. He caught her hips with one hand on each side and pounded forward, stroking into her with all the marvel and delight of a sixteen-year-old with his first girl.

Rebecca wailed again, high and long, like a she-lion in heat. It only whetted his performance, and he speeded up his motions. This was one position he knew let him strike her tiny clit and pound her toward her own climax.

Rebecca's passion built and built. Trembling and crying out, she looked back at him, nodding, and at last she let out such a wail of success that he wondered if the train whistle had sounded.

Her whole body rattled and shook and vibrated like a thousand loose ties, and she bucked and jolted so hard he had trouble staying with her. Three times she went through the ritual of a female climax, and all the time Aaron stroked into her heartland.

Just before her final shout of glory, Aaron felt his own climax pounding through his body and slammed her harder until he drove her forward and she fell on her stomach on the hay, where he stretched out over the top of her, still connected.

"If you move within the next ten minutes, I'll push you out of the car door," she said softly. He chuckled, but he didn't move.

The ten minutes were almost up when they sensed the train slowing. There were two train whistle blasts, and then all of the cars lurched as the engineer started applying the brakes.

They rolled apart and quickly adjusted their clothes. She slipped on her bloomers, chemise and blouse, and Aaron looked out the train car door.

"Water stop ahead. Guess this will be a good chance to go back to the passenger car unless you like it here better."

Rebecca hadn't quite come down off her emotional high, but she snorted. "You know I like it here better, but I guess we should go back."

She stood and picked up her gunbelt with the twin .44 Smith and Wesson American revolvers in it that she had carried with her from the passenger car. It

25

wouldn't look right strapped around her traveling dress. At least she had the weapons.

The train rolled slower and slower and stopped. They were at the door when they heard the first shot. A trainman at the water tank crumpled and dropped on the tracks ahead.

As they watched, a man led six horses across the tracks. The water spout was not down. A trainman jumped down from the engine, and another man followed him, holding a gun on the man she now saw was the engineer.

"Come on!" Rebecca called and jumped down from the livestock car and ran forward. They bent and looked under the car and could see three more horses rush up to the other side of the train.

"There's a Railway Express car up front, and I saw some guards before we left Flag. This train came from San Francisco. Might be mint gold on board and somebody is looking to make a big haul."

"Let's move up there through the passenger cars," Aaron whispered. He led the way. They went up the steps and into the small vestibule between the cars. For a moment all was quiet. Then gunfire sounded again, inside or outside the car—they didn't know which.

Marshall Aaron Hawkins quietly opened the door into the car ahead and stepped in. Two men at the far end of the car wore masks. They waved their guns as they yelled something at the passengers.

Rebecca stepped up beside Aaron, her right hand aiming one of the big American .44's.

"Drop it!" Aaron barked.

The gunmen looked up, and when both turned, one of them lost his mask; and Rebecca saw a face that looked so shrunken it seemed to be a skull. Both the outlaws fired at almost the same time. Aaron got off one shot, and Rebecca fired as well. She could feel the bullets hit Aaron. He jolted backward against the

26

door and rammed it open before he fell on his back into the vestibule.

She crawled after him and found him on his back, his chest smeared with blood. Quickly she lifted his head to her lap.

He looked at her and shivered. "We had good times," Aaron said; then his eyes closed with agonizing slowness, and she heard the last gush of air that would ever come from his lungs.

"Bastards!" Rebecca screamed. She gently laid his head on the hard steel, picked up her hogleg in her right hand and opened the door into the train with her left. Aaron was dead, and somebody was going to pay for it!

At the other end of the car, she saw one of the outlaws lying in the aisle between the seats. Aaron's shot had hit its mark. No one else was visible for a moment. The passengers had all slid down behind the seats or crouched on the floor. The other outlaw had retreated.

Rebecca stepped silently into the car and crouched behind the nearest seat. She peered over the top of it at the far vestibule. She thought she could see men through the glass door.

A moment later the skull-faced man and two others came into the car and stared at their fallen outlaw. The one with the skull-like face fired once into the roof. When the roaring sound faded, the skull face shouted at them.

"This is a holdup. We want all of your valuables, now!" He jerked a hat off a passenger and held it out.

Men began putting wallets into the hat. Women put in rings and necklaces. A small redheaded Irish mother clutched her two daughters to her breast and at the same time held on to her purse.

"No, no! It's all the money we have in the world."

The skull-faced man grabbed at the purse, but she clung to it.

"No!" she screamed.

The skull-faced man had a long skinny neck, a large nose, deep-sunken black eyes and cheeks shrunken to the point of emaciation. His dark eyes glinted as he frowned. Then he laughed and shot the redheaded woman in the forehead. She jolted against the seat back, and the small girls screamed. The skull-faced man bellowed in rage and shot both the girls in the chest.

Through a thick cloud of blue smoke from the rounds, he grabbed the purse and threw it behind him to another robber.

Rebecca trembled with rage. She didn't have a good shot at him yet. One old man in front of her had stood, evidently trying to hear what the robbers were saying.

A third gunman moved in front of the skull-faced man, waving his revolver.

"That's what happens when you don't cooperate. So, just hand it over folks, all of it, and no one else gets hurt." This outlaw had a kerchief mask covering his face below his eyes.

"Lots easier to replace a few trinkets and dollars than it is to pay for a funeral. Come on now, don't be bashful. Rings, watches and cash."

The man held out a high-crowned cowboy hat for the contributions.

Thirty feet away, Rebecca moved into the aisle. When the bandit turned her way and looked at her, she shot him in the chest with the heavy .44 slug. He screeched in anger and agony, then slid to the floor and died.

The two outlaws behind him, including the scarecrow of a man, fired past their dying buddy. They missed because Rebecca had dropped behind one of the empty seats. Then the robbers ran for the far door and crouched behind the partition. Rebecca darted behind the cover of the vestibule door and waited.

Soon a shot came from down the aisle toward Rebecca's direction but hit the overhead steel and dropped to the floor.

She heard some loud talk from the pair at the far end of the car. A baby halfway down began to cry, but a frantic mother opened her blouse and suckled the child to quiet it. A woman whimpered, and her husband comforted her.

"Give it up and get off the car or I'll come down there and gut shoot both of you!" Rebecca called.

Her warning brought a mirthless laugh as an arm stretched around the partition with a six-gun ready to fire. Rebecca's round struck first, slashing upward along the gunman's arm, shattering the smaller bone, then exiting through the complicated tendon and bone juncture at his elbow. The arm vanished behind the partition and was followed by a scream of pain. She heard hurried steps as the gunmen left the train.

Rebecca ran up the pullman aisle and checked the second gunman on the floor. He was dead. She took his six-gun, an old Colt Peacemaker .45 fully loaded, and gave the hat to the people who had been robbed. Then she ran back to the door from which she had come.

No one challenged her as she peered out, then stepped to the ground and ran forward toward the special car from San Francisco. She saw that it was a Railway Express car. Before she reached it, a blast on the other side of the train shook the express car, and she saw a rising column of smoke.

Dust and more smoke billowed from under the car, blinding her for a moment. When she could see again, Rebecca noticed the sliding door in the middle of the Railway Express car on her side begin to open.

She heard gunfire from the other side of the car and now held the two revolvers aimed at the door. It slammed fully open, and two men jumped out, each with a heavy bag marked "U.S. Mint."

"Hold it!" she yelled. They looked up at her as they landed from the three-foot jump, shrugged and ran down the easy slope of the roadbed. She shot one in the shoulder and the other in the legs, and both went down.

"Don't touch your iron or you're dead men," she barked, then looked back at the door in time to see a shotgun pointing at her. Her right hand snapped two quick shots at a fat-cheeked man holding a scatter gun. One round rook him in the side of the head and drove him back, dead, into the car. The Greener fell to the tracks and discharged, showering double-aught buck rounds down the rails.

Rebecca ducked back against the side of the car and waited. The two men on the right-of-way below began to edge hands toward their weapons. She shot the closest man in the thigh, and he bellowed in fury and pain.

"Stay!" she brayed, and this time they did.

She heard horses on the other side of the tracks, followed by a shower of shotgun and rifle rounds; then she moved away from the heavy steel wheels of the train and looked under the car. She could see three horses riding hard away from the site.

Rebecca stayed where she was.

A voice sounded inside the car, then another. The men talked in normal tones; then a head poked out of the car and back in at once. One of the voices came louder.

"Hey, outside. Do we have a friendly gun out there?"

"Hey, inside. You with the bad guys or the good guys?"

A laugh billowed from the car. "Be damned, a woman. You the one who's got those two jaspers out in the ditch under your gun?"

"Might be. Who are you?"

"Kennedy, Secret Service. Working this easy trip from San Francisco to Santa Fe with gold coins for the banks; then we turn south into Texas."

"Sounds right. Rebecca Caldwell here. If you want these two malcontents out there in the ditch, come and get them."

The same head came out and looked toward her voice. "Miss Caldwell, mighty glad you came along. You saved our bacon in here. That one guy with the shotgun had us dead as a doornail before you blew his head off. My wife and three kids in San Francisco thank you."

He jumped out of the car then, and she saw he was lean and tall, with a shotgun of his own now aimed at the two in the ditch. He motioned, and another man jumped from the express car and worked his way down the low embankment to the two outlaws.

He carefully stripped the guns from them, then marched them back to the express car and made them climb in by themselves. Both yelled and complained about their wounds.

The first government agent went down and brought back the two sacks of gold coins. He made two trips. After he pushed the second bag of coins into the express car, he grinned.

"Three hundred gold double eagles in each bag. That's six thousand dollars' worth. The robbers almost made it."

"Sounds like an elaborate setup. Who's robbing trains with that kind of organization around here?"

"We're not sure, but in this area, we always think about *el Zopilote.*"

"The Buzzard? I've heard of him. He operates out of Taos if I remember right."

"True. I got a good look at one of the men who came boiling out of your passenger car. He was one of the Buzzard's top lieutenants. He's skinny and has a face like a skull and a body like a skeleton. We call

31

him the Chicken. He's deadly, but something sure put a fire on his tail today."

"That was me. Four of them came into the car I was in to rob the passengers. The Chicken killed my long-time friend, Marshall Aaron Hawkins of Flagstaff. The bastard skull-faced man then murdered a woman and her two small daughters for no reason at all. I've got a score with them, especially that skull-faced man."

"They didn't profit a dollar on the raid. We killed three of them, captured two. We've got six horses back in the cattle car and a tracker. In a few minutes, we're heading out after those three who got away, including the Chicken."

"I hope you catch them. If you don't, I'll be on their trail after my business is over in Santa Fe."

"Thanks, we'll get the train going as soon as we can."

Rebecca went back to the passenger car she had left, and a dozen people came up to her to thank her for saving their money and valuables. The bodies of the two outlaws, and those of the Irish woman and her two small daughters, had already been taken from the car.

Aaron lay where he had fallen. Rebecca sat down on the steel plates beside him and scowled at the conductor when he came with the brakeman. They retreated, giving her a few more minutes with all that remained of one of her best friends.

The conductor came through saying they would be moving in another two or three minutes, as soon as they got the water they had stopped here for.

Rebecca stayed with Aaron, remembering all of the good times. They were less than two hours from Santa Fe. She wondered why *el Zopilote* had sent men way down here, but knew the answer at once. The train probably carried fifty thousand dollars' worth of gold coins. A fabulous target for any bandit. But this time there was a well-armed guard force.

She had to stop in Santa Fe. The dead were dead and could wait. The killer would get away; this was his country. She would find him in Taos. First she would comfort the living, and then go after the man who killed Aaron. *She would find him and kill him!*

Soon she would be in Santa Fe, one of her favorite towns. She nodded, closed her eyes, then snapped them open at once, the memory of the gunman shooting down Aaron was suddenly more terrible than she could stand.

She stroked Aaron's hair, moved it out of his eyes, then stood and paced the aisle while the conductor and the brakeman quietly removed the body of her dead friend. By the time the train began to move, Rebecca Caldwell had worked out her plan. She would stop in Santa Fe for a day at the most, then go on to Taos by stagecoach and dig out this *el Zopilote* and punish him for the death of Aaron and those three innocents. She'd start with the skull-faced Chicken and then get *el Zopilote*. Yes, it would be done!

CHAPTER 3

Eugenio Gomez pulled up his horse and studied the train behind him. They were taking on water. It would be moving soon. He cursed and shouted at the train. It had been a big fat cow waiting to be slaughtered. Now most of his men were dead or captured. What had gone so wrong? How had he failed so miserably?

He knew. It was that white bitch! That half-breed whore! He recognized her, the White Squaw, Rebecca Caldwell. He had seen her before, but she hadn't remembered him. Now he had to get back to Taos and report to *el Zopilote*. It would not be easy.

As he stared at the train, he saw a door roll open on a cattle car and four horsemen jump horses out of the car and charge straight for them.

"Amigos, vamonos!" He pointed at the horses. He and his men would be able to outwit and outride the *gringos*. Still it could be close. They had not more than a half mile head start. But they had to get away. No matter what the American *federales* did, Eugenio knew that he had to get back to the Buzzard. He would not be happy, but at least he would know that the *gringa blanco* was in the area; perhaps she would try to find them in Taos.

He pointed his mount north into some scrub pine

and on into the heavier timbered slopes. It would be harder to track them in the timber. As soon as they hit the denser growth, all three of them would take different tracks, heading in different directions and splitting the force behind them. Then any confrontation would be easier.

As he rode hard into the brush and trees, Eugenio, the Chicken, tried to figure out what had gone wrong at the train. They had captured the engine, blown the door off the treasure car, had three men inside and gotten out with at least two bags of gold.

It had to have been that half-breed Sioux bitch, Caldwell. How could she be everywhere at once? She had killed Rodolfo in the passenger car and fired at him. He had seen her gun down his two men outside; then Pepe, with the shotgun in the express car, had lost his face and his life from her guns. Eugenio shook his head, checked behind him and spurred his horse like the devil himself was riding on his tail.

Joel Carson sat back in the big leather executive chair at the head of the table in the boardroom in the tallest building in Denver and listened to the discussion. The proposal was to buy up the stock of a rival mining company and slowly take over the firm without them knowing it.

"By the time we have twenty percent of their stock, we'll be in a position to dictate certain staff changes and management changes," Clint Linderston said softly. "They never will be able to get a majority of the stockholders to vote together. We buy out another thirty-one percent and merge the firm with our own, or simply run it as a subsidiary."

Joel glanced at Linderston. He and Linderston had been gently promoting this idea for a month, but didn't want to seem to be forcing it down the throats of the other men on the board.

Not that they could be outvoted. Joel owned fifty-two percent of the Carson Mining Company Inc., and in the last ten years he had amassed a fortune worth well over twenty million dollars.

His father had given him twenty thousand dollars on his twenty-first birthday and told him to go make his own fortune. Joel's father had become wealthy in Boston in the shipping trade and enjoyed life and had no thought for his son to follow in the shipping business.

Joel had come to Denver, bought a store, and doubled the profits the first year. The next year he bought half of a mine that was in trouble financially. He turned it around and soon owned all of it, then hit a new gold vein. From there on everything he bought turned into gold, and now, at the age of thirty-four, he was one of the richest men in Denver. He had never married, but not because half of the eligible young women in Denver didn't court him.

Now he played with the company more than anything. His most enjoyable avocation lay in quite another direction.

The conversation about the stock plan droned on. Then suddenly, and to his surprise, the strongest holdout on the buy-out scheme switched sides and called for a vote. The move to buy the stock of Wonderland Mining and Smeltering passed unanimously.

Joel adjourned the board meeting and went back to his big office on the same floor. He had a corner suite that showed off most of Denver to the north and the mountains in the distance. He never tired of watching them.

Milly, his long-time secretary and office manager, came in with a fresh cup of coffee and a Danish sweet roll with cinnamon and walnuts for him, which she carefully set on his desk.

"You asked me to remind you about your run this

36

afternoon. Is it true that you want to try for the Olympics this coming year?"

"Milly, you are giving me ideas. I think the mile would be my best bet, don't you?" They both chuckled. It was her little campaign for him to stay fit and trim. She had gently scolded him lately because he had put on five pounds.

"We received another wire from Miles City, Montana. It seems they are extremely interested in Ned Silver coming there to help them settle some problem with rustlers."

"Yes, Montana." He settled down in a big over-stuffed chair which rocked and also swiveled. He'd had it made to order. He slipped off his shoes and put his stockinged feet up on an ottoman.

Milly started to hand him the coffee, but he waved her aside and picked his cup up off his desk and swiveled around.

"Milly, wire them back and say that Ned Silver is currently overloaded with responsibilities and can't in good conscience come to Miles City." He frowned. "That's not more than a very small white lie. Actually it's the coming winter there. If Ned started now, it would surely snow before the project was through. While we do get some snow here, it's nothing like the wilds of Montana."

"I'll see that it gets off today, sir."

"Milly, isn't tonight the opera?"

"Yes, sir, one of your favorites by a traveling troupe. It's said to be quite good, although the orchestra leaves something to be desired."

"One of the drawbacks of living in the splendor of Denver, my dear lady. We can't summon up the New York Philharmonic Orchestra to play for every opera troupe that comes to town. Oh, you better send a messenger around to Miss Millford's residence re-minding her of our engagement tonight for dinner at six and then the opera. Tell her I'll pick her up

37

promptly at five-forty-five."

"Yes, Mr. Carson."

"Ah ha. I've finally found a young lady of which you approve."

"Yes, sir. She's a jewel, and one who won't last long in this bachelor-ridden city. If I might be so bold . . ." She looked up, and his wry grin told her that she should not be quite that bold.

"Very well, Mr. Carson, I'll send the note around promptly."

She left the room, and Joel checked the appointment pad in front of him on the large, sleek cherrywood desk. The desk was flat on top, not cluttered with a roll top, and had two neat stacks of papers. One was marked "To Do." The other stack was under a note on the desk in Milly's handwriting that said, "Sometime." He looked at the to do stack, then checked the time and hurried through a door from the office into his five-room apartment. He took a hot bath, then dressed casually and hurried downstairs and walked up two blocks to the Alhambra Tonsorial Parlor.

He was expected.

"Mr. Carson. We've had a chair just waiting for you. Shampoo first before the haircut?"

"Yes, Mr. Alhambra, the usual."

"Everything?"

"The works."

First came the hair wash with some French shampoo specially scented and guaranteed to result in more manageable hair, then the trim as two assistants swept up every clip and dark lock that hit the floor.

"Your usual businessman's cut, Mr. Carson?"

"The usual. Then a manicure, a close shave and that famous neck and back massage of yours. I've had a hard day at the office."

38

"Exactly, Mr. Carson. Is it the opera tonight?"

"Exactly, Mr. Alhambra."

"Who is the lucky lady?"

"I can't tell you, because you might try to beat my time with her."

They both laughed. It was a small ritual they went through nearly every time he came in. Usually he arrived once a week for the works. He had been having his hair cut here for the past ten years.

That evening, Joel Carson arrived at the stately home of Miss Annabelle Millford at precisely five-forty-five. She wasn't ready, and they finally left in his carriage at six-fifteen.

Annabelle was soft and short and slender, with a fine smile and perfect manners. Sleek, blond hair halfway down her back and vivid blue eyes helped, but he just couldn't get excited about this girl. Too much polish, not enough substance.

They had supper at one of the fine restaurants in Denver, Claudine's. He paid the tab of almost eleven dollars. *Ridiculous*, he fumed to himself. *That was more money than a working man makes all week. Ought to be a law against high-priced restaurants.*

The opera put him in a better mood. It was Verdi's recent opera which had its debut in Cairo for the opening of the Suez Canal. It was *Aida*, and Joel soon agreed with Milly that the orchestra was the weakest part of the local production. But the songs!

He dropped the slightly depressed Miss Millford off at her house with only a good-night kiss on the cheek and hurried back to his suite of rooms high in the Carson Building.

A note had been left on his pillow, by Milly, he was sure. Inside the envelope he found a telegram from Santa Fe, New Mexico. He read it under the flare of the gas light.

39

Mr. Joel Carson, Carson Building, Denver, Colorado.

Mr. Carson. If you could put me in contact with one Ned Silver, I would be most appreciative. We have a growing troublesome situation here in Taos that I wish to speak with Mr. Silver about.

I don't have authorization yet from the city council, but we are contemplating engaging Mr. Silver to "clean house" in our town and set to right law and order and bring the three elements of the town together that are now tearing it apart. I refer to the white settlers, the entrenched Mexicans and the long-time residents, the Tewa and other elements of the Pueblo Indian tribes.

I would appreciate your consideration in contacting Mr. Silver for us, and ascertaining his availability for an engagement here as soon as possible. Confirmation of this offer to follow along with the fee we can pay. Please respond by wire to Santa Fe, where the message will be forwarded to us by stage.

Your obedient servant, Webb Bryce, Chairman of the Taos City Council.

Joel Carson read the telegram again and thought about it as he undressed and dropped into bed. Taos in the fall might be nice. He'd wait and see what the city council decided. He was pretty sure that he could locate Ned Silver if he had to.

In Santa Fe, Rebecca Caldwell took a room at the New Mexican Hotel, the best one in town, had a long, relaxing bath in a tub brought right to her room, then stretched out on her bed to consider her next step.

In Santa Fe lived one of her mother's closest friends. They had been in school together and had both married early and lived on nearby farms for several years.

Now the woman was here in Santa Fe. Her husband had died some years before, leaving her a sizeable fortune. She stayed here now and amused herself with establishing a city library and badgering the city and rich men in town to contribute to it. Twice Rebecca had been here to see her. She was starting to fail. Her hearing was poor and her eyesight dim.

Rebecca called on Hattie Handshoe that evening. The woman wasn't that old, about the same age Rebecca's mother would have been, fifty-one. The servant brought her into the big house's own library, and Hattie rose to meet her guest.

Tears slipped down her cheeks as she watched the young woman walk across the imported carpet.

"Rebecca!" She wiped her eyes with a linen handkerchief. "It's always a miracle and I thank the Lord for it every time I see you. To think what you've gone through, and now you're so strong and serene. It's a miracle of our Lord Jesus, I'm sure."

They embraced, and Rebecca dried the tears from the older woman's face.

"You're looking so well, Aunt Hattie," Rebecca said. She had always called the woman "aunt." Early on the pioneer farm the women had decided it wasn't necessary for the children to use the title missus, but it wasn't polite to use first names, either. So the families in the area had had their children call the adult women "aunt." It satisfied everyone.

"Well? No child, not well, but as good as can be expected. Every day I say a prayer for your mother. She should be here with me, enjoying the good life. Instead . . . instead—"

Rebecca knew her aunt Hattie would do it again.

41

"How your uncles could ever sell you and your mother into slavery to the Oglala Sioux is totally beyond my ability to understand. How they could barter you for their freedom. Then you had to spend the next four years of your life as a captive slave of the ferocious Sioux Indians!" Aunt Hattie shivered.

"I understand that you are the product of a savage attack by Iron Calf against your mother during a raid of the farm many years before. But then for your mother to be held as a slave of the Sioux! Disgusting, terrible. They are truly savages. No wonder your dear mother went mad and died there in that heathen camp."

Hattie took deep breaths and looked faint, but she held on. Rebecca put her arm around her. "Now, Aunt Hattie, you're not supposed to think about that. It all happened so many years ago, and now we're here and we're happy and well; and I hope that you're still working to establish a strong Santa Fe city library."

The talk shifted then, and Rebecca was no longer as glad that she had come as she had been. It was a duty call, and as long as this woman lived, Rebecca would visit her, and care for her if it came to that.

They had dinner together that evening. Even in Santa Fe they were calling the night meal dinner now instead of supper. But it would take a long time to fade out the farm-related term of supper. They ate in the formal dining room, and Aunt Hattie's cook served up a remarkable meal.

Then they talked more in the library. Every few minutes Rebecca's thoughts would flash back to the death of Aaron Hawkins, and she shivered in anger. She was wasting time here in Santa Fe. Then she remembered how much Aunt Hattie enjoyed the visits, and she stayed awhile longer. At last the urge was too strong. She still felt close to Aaron. It had been such a wonderful relationship. She wouldn't

42

rest until his killers were dead.

"Aunt Hattie, I really better go. I have a ride on the stage for Taos that leaves a little after seven tomorrow morning. I better get some sleep or I'll miss the last call."

"Taos? Why for heaven's sake would you go up there in the mountains to that little Indian town?"

"I have some business up there, Aunt Hattie. Some business that really can't wait." Never had Rebecca let this frail, delicate woman know about her activities. Aunt Hattie would have been surprised and probably shocked at how Rebecca lived her life. Even knowing that she had at last paid back her two uncles who sold her into slavery might not sit well with the older woman.

Aunt Hattie had her driver get out the rig and take Rebecca the four blocks to the center of town and the hotel.

"I don't want some nere-do-well to accost you on the street this late at night," Aunt Hattie said.

Rebecca started to tell her that was not necessary, but she remained quiet, projecting her soft, shy help-less-woman impression to the older woman. What could it hurt.

The next morning, Rebecca packed away her pretty, girlish dresses, put on a brown shirt, a brown pair of pants, sturdy half-boots and strapped on her two loaded Smith and Wesson American .44's. At the stage station, she bought a ticket to Taos. She had only one big leather suitcase, which was heavy because she had a disassembled rifle in there and a sawed-off shotgun. She was eager to see what she could find in Taos.

CHAPTER 4

Gray Squirrel shifted in his position in front of a small fire near the clap of his traveling tipi which had been put up on the very edge of the recently restored chief of chiefs' burial grounds. The tipi cover was made from light buffalo hides from calves and smaller cows that he had received from the plains Indians in trade for horses.

He sat cross-legged and watched the elderly Indian beside him, the dauntless and much respected Two Feathers, the shaman of their tribe of Taos Pueblo Indians.

They spoke softly in the Pfia, or feather clan, language. This ages-old Tewa speech came down to them over the centuries. One day, a Chinese man traveling through Taos had listened to two Tewa Indians talking. He had been totally enraptured by the speech, saying that he could understand little of it, but it was so much like his native Chinese that he thought he was home again.

He had explained to the mayor of Taos that the Pfia language made use of tones much like Chinese did and seemed to have forty-five distinct sounds. The musical accents of the Pfia language were identical to those of Chinese, and so were most of the sounds.

Now Gray Squirrel stared at the restored land that had been snatched back from the whites who wanted to build a warehouse there and put a cover over most of the ancient graves. All of the sacred circle stones had been disrupted and pushed aside and even picked up and thrown into a pile at the far end of the lot.

Six Indian men under the shaman's direction had been sorting out the stones and returning them to their rightful circles according to the rank and age of the buried chiefs. It was all spelled out by the size, color and age of the rocks, and only the shaman could decipher them.

Two Feathers looked up from a small bowl he had been eating from. "What can we do to keep the white men from defiling our sacred ground?" Two Feathers asked his leader.

Gray Squirrel shifted on the small buffalo robe where he sat. The bone-madness afflicted him again. His joints did not wish to work right when he arose in the morning. Some of his bones hurt all day. Wet times were the worst. He thanked the great spirit that in Taos Pueblo there were few days of rain.

His gnarled, forty-five-year-old hands rubbed his eyes. It was the plains Indians' sign for crying. "Holy man, we can cry a lot. It will do no good unless the Taos work together and make big talk with the whites and the Mexicans. We are a peaceful people. It takes a great deal to anger us to the point of taking up the spear and bow and painting our faces black.

"We have taught the rivers and streams to do our bidding. We shift them and channel them and move their waters to where our eager crops await. For more than a dozen sons of sons, it has been so. We have been overrun by the Spaniards with their metal breastplates and their 7-dogs the whites call horses.

"We kept the 7-dogs and now trade them to many of our brothers in the plains. But we rose up and killed the treacherous Spaniards and drove their men

45

and their priests and their soldiers and their religion out of the valley."

Two Feathers lifted his hand, stood from his cross-legged position without the use of his hands, lifting up quickly and straight. He went to one of the circles of rocks the men had finished.

From a pouch under his dark doe-skin shirt, he took out a pinch of cornmeal and threw it to the east, where the glorious sun rose each morning. Then he tossed a pinch of the cornmeal to each of the other three main compass points, chanting softly prayers for the departed, and prayers that their spirits had escaped their bodies and were friends of everyone in the place of many spirits.

He returned and sat, finished eating from the bowl and stared at the half-ruined pueblo buildings.

"We could bring two or three families to live in the old pueblo and act as guards over the graves," Two Feathers said. "It is sad. In the old days the white eyes and the Mexicans respected our sacred ground."

"We must remind them. We will build a platform of the dead here between the rock circles. It will be enough to show the others that this is indeed sacred land."

Two hours later, six Indians brought in loads of sticks and hatchets, and quickly set about building a platform six feet long and two feet wide. It was made of sticks tied together with grass and supported by bound-together bundles of small branches so it rested three feet off the ground. Over it was a roof made of twigs and branches and covered with dry grass fastened in bundles and then tied to the network on the roof. As three black and white eagle feathers were positioned on the top of the shelter, the two older Indians stood and began to walk toward their pueblo.

The six Taos Tewa Indians finished the shelter and turned just as a white man came running to the

46

edge of the sacred ground.

"What the hell's going on?" he shouted. He lifted a six-gun and aimed it at the closest Indian worker.

"What you doing on my land?" the white man bellowed. "I'm Maxwell Montrose, and I own this land. Gonna build me a new warehouse here whether you damned heathens want me to or not."

The Indian looked at the white man and shrugged. He did not understand the English words.

"Bastard!" Montrose snarled. He fired one shot from the revolver, and the Tewa Indian jolted backward, then stumbled and fell to the ground. He never moved again.

Webb Bryce ran up and grabbed the six-gun from the freight line owner. "Montrose, I told you we'd take care of it. It's going to take a little more time. Now you've done it. You better pray that Indian isn't dead. If he is, we got more trouble on our hands than we can take care of."

As soon as they heard the yelling behind them, Gray Squirrel and Two Feathers turned. They stared in amazement, then horror as the white man fired his weapon.

Two Feathers rushed to the downed man. He lifted the brave's head and laid it in his lap and stared into his eyes. Then he touched the fallen warrior's chest but could feel no heartbeat. He closed the brave's eyelids, and they stayed closed.

"Muerte!" Two Feathers said, using the Mexican word he had learned many years ago. "Our friend Red Willow is dead. We must prepare for the ceremony of the yet undeparted warrior's spirit."

An hour later it began in the Taos *kiva*. This ceremonial room had been built in the old fashion, twenty feet long and ten feet wide, and dug into the pliant soil under the seven-story pueblo near where

47

the stream gushed down from Glorietta Canyon.

There were two pyramids that made up the Taos pueblo. One held terraced houses made of the traditional adobe bricks that reached up seven stories at the top. The other one was five rooms high.

The first floor had no doors or windows. A ladder made of sturdy poles with holes dug through each side to hold the rungs led to the flat top of the first-floor structure. Here another ladder provided a way downward into the first-floor rooms. The arrangement helped in the defense of the pueblo. When enemies threatened, the Indians ran up the ladders, then pulled them up behind them, creating an automatic defensive eight-foot wall to deter the invaders.

The pueblos were constructed so that the roof of one floor of dwellings became the terraced "front yard" of the story above it. It was here that much of the work of drying and shelling and preparing their crops was done.

No one could remember how long the Tewa people had been in Taos. Some of the old rolls of deer skins that had the picture history on them took the present Indians back well into fifteen generations. One or two pictures were drawn on the skins each year to commemorate the most important happenings of that year.

The Tewas' history was also passed on orally as a father told his son the ancient stories. They were repeated so often and with such enthusiasm that soon the children had the stories memorized with no special effort. When they had children, they would work the magic again to preserve the history of the Tewa people.

The ritual of the dead would begin in the *kiva*, the holy place where many of the Pueblo Indians' ceremonies took place. The *kiva* had been dug into the ground below the largest set of rooms in the center of

48

the pueblo. This protected it. In the times of the Spanish rulers, it also served to hide the ceremonials from the Spanish and keep the old ways pure and safe during the long years of Spanish oppression.

Gray Squirrel watched as the body of the man was lowered through the door into the *kiva*, then he put on his ceremonial shirt of white buckskin and climbed down the ladder into the room. It was time for the ceremony to begin.

"Damn fool!" Webb Bryce thundered as he towered over Maxwell Montrose. The man sat in the saloon and belted down a shot of whiskey before he looked up.

"Hell, he was trespassing on my property and I shot him. My right. Damn savage shouldn't been there. I need that warehouse. First, three of my best teamsters get shot down, murdered on the street, and now this happens. Webb! What the hell we gonna do now?"

"I don't know. But one thing we better do is try to make amends somehow for that brave you killed."

"How?"

"First thing you do is buy six steers and drive them up there to that widow squaw and give them to her. Then you buy yourself fifty bushels of good, dry shelled corn and take that up to her. You get that done today while they're away having their burial ceremony, and maybe, just maybe, they won't come down here and slice you into about three hundred pieces."

Acting Sheriff Quint Wonlander stood watching Montrose. "Hell, Max, I think you better do like Webb here says. No law around here against killing Indians. Problem is you're upsetting a shaky truce we have with them bastards. They don't like us, and most of us hate them; but we got to live with them.

49

Still more of them out there than there are of us—we got to live with that for damn sure."

Montrose stood and held on to the saloon table. "All right, damn it, all right! I'll get some beef and corn for the squaw. How am I supposed to know which one she is?"

"They'll figure it out," Webb said. "Better get your ass moving 'fore we have an Indian uprising."

A man ran in the saloon. He looked around, spotted the lawman and hurried over.

"You best get out here, Sheriff. We got some more trouble. One of the Mexes is in a knife fight with an Injun. Both of them blooded already."

The four men hurried outside. Twenty yards down the street, two men faced each other on the board-walk. The Tewa Indian had dropped the white cotton blanket that had been wrapped around his waist and hanging down around his knees. It had looked like a skirt before he stripped it off. Now he wore only the traditional Indian breechclout. His bronze bare body weaved back and forth in a half crouch, arms held out at the ready in front of him, a six-inch skinning knife in his right hand, a four-inch blade in his left. He held both by the handles with the blades pointing straight ahead. It gave him the advantage of stabbing or slashing with the blade in any direction.

Across from him a Mexican man about twenty years old stared in anger at the four-inch slice on the top of his left arm. He had a knife in his right hand but nothing in his left.

The sheriff fired twice into the air with his double-action six-gun, and both fighters looked at him.

"Stop it! *Alto de aqui!*" the acting sheriff bellowed. "What's going on here?"

The Indian looked at the sheriff, then at his revolver that now pointed between the two combatants.

"That's enough, Eulogio, put it away and get out

50

of here." The Mexican man stared at the sheriff for a moment, then grabbed the wound on his arm and ran down the street.

The Indian saw him leave and slowly dropped his arms. He slid the knives back in soft leather scabbards, then looked at the sheriff. For a moment his eyes stared straight at Montrose, then he turned and ran between the buildings and toward the pueblo.

"Not bad, Sheriff," Webb said. "I've got a feeling that young Injun was wanting Montrose's blood on his knife. He must be related to the brave Montrose killed a couple of hours ago. Word travels fast in the pueblo."

"My God, you've got to protect me!" Montrose squealed.

Webb snorted. "Buy yourself another gun, Montrose. I've got to get to the special city council meeting."

Five minutes later, Webb saw that this time all five of the men of the council were in their chairs.

"So what are we going to do?" Webb asked.

Lynn Keating, the man missing at the first session, looked around the group. "What did you talk about this morning?"

"Damn little," Josh Randall said. "We waited for you. Got to have all five of us here."

"Tell you what I'd do if somebody tried to rustle some of my stock, or squatters moved in on my grass," Keating said. He ran the LK brand Keating Ranch five miles out of town.

"We can guess what you'd do, Lynn, but we can't do that. Let's get serious. There are more than two hundred Taos Indians up there. Pueblo, Tewas, whatever you want to call them. They can send runners out to twenty more pueblos around this area and pour two thousand warriors in here hunting for blood. We're not looking for a massacre."

"You know Maxwell Montrose just killed one of their men," Josh Randall said. "Got liquored up and

51

went out and shot him down in front of fifty people."

"Is it gonna explode on us?" Ingemar Olson asked. He ran the Taos barbershop and used to sew up cuts and dig out bullets before the doctor came to town.

"Not if we take care of it," Webb said. "Montrose is sending up some cattle and corn to the widow. Now, what we gonna do about the damn property where the burial ground is?"

"Who sold Montrose the property?" Olson asked. "Why did the first man think he owned it?"

Webb motioned to their secretary and sent her down to the courthouse to find out who the former owners of that corner lot were.

"Maybe it's time we get ourselves a town tamer," Webb said. "I hear there's a good one in Denver. A gent named Ned Silver."

"He's a gunsharp!" Randall said. "Probably wind up gunning down half the people in town."

"Not so," Webb countered. "I've had some good reports on him from around the country. He's good with a gun, but he's also honest and has a healthy respect for the law. There's a rumor going around that he's more than just a gunman, but I can't pin that down. I'm in favor of pulling him in here to settle down this whole thing. We've got everybody fighting everybody else."

"We ever find out who killed them three teamsters the other night?"

"Not so far," Webb said. "They were all shot, and bullets don't talk. Interesting part is that none of them were robbed. So it was an angry killing. Somebody killing out of principle maybe."

"That's just part of our troubles," Lynn Keating said. "That damn self-styled Mexican colonel is talking big again. Sure, sure, I know he's a businessman here, rich and has a lot of friends. But I don't trust him."

"El Zopilote," the barber said. "I cut the colonel's hair now and then, and I still say that Colonel

Antonio Sinfuegos and this Mexican outlaw, The Buzzard, are one and the same man."

Webb waved away cigar smoke from Randall's stogie. "If that's true, then we have even more cause to bring in a man like Ned Silver. How much could we offer him if we want to ask him to come down here? He's just up in Denver."

"Do we need a town tamer?" Owen Johnson asked. Owen was a lawyer, and had most of the business in Taos since he was the only legal mind in town.

"What do you think, Owen? Four murders in less than twenty-four hours." Josh Randall said it.

They talked for a half hour, then took a vote. It was four to one for someone to approach Ned Silver.

"I know the name of a man in Denver who can contact Silver," Webb said. "Of course, he might be on another job somewhere."

"Send him a wire with the stage driver," Josh said. "Most of the drivers from here will hand carry a telegram to the office in Santa Fe for two dollars."

"Done," Webb said. The meeting broke up, and Webb Bryce headed for the stage depot to write out a telegram for the morning driver to take to the telegraph office. The city council had decided it would offer Silver three thousand dollars for the job. It wouldn't be a lot of money to Silver, but it was a year's wages for a cowhand, or a miner, or a clerk in a store.

In the telegram, Webb added that Silver was authorized to bring along ten "Regulators" of his own choosing. The city would pay them two dollars a day if they worked no more than thirty days. That could be another six hundred dollars the city was spending.

Webb shrugged. If nine hundred dollars could save the town from turning into a shooting war and stop an Indian uprising, it would be worth it.

CHAPTER 5

Eugenio and the two surviving members of his band had ridden hard for two days after that futile attack on the treasure train and reached Taos about midday. He stabled his horse, washed his face and hands and combed his hair. Only then did he go up the long block through what had become the Mexican section of Taos.

Nobody had planned it that way. The Mexican people had simply moved together for convenience and protection. Half a block from the big house of Colonel Sinfuegos, a sentry left the shade of a house and came toward the man with the skull-like face. He carried a revolver in leather at his hip and a sullen expression.

"Where you going?" the man asked Eugenio.

"To see the colonel. You're new here. I'm Eugenio Gomez."

"Give me your *pistola* and we will see. They told me nothing about a Gomez coming."

"At least the security is as good as ever. I began with the colonel as a guard."

They went into the house with the shade, through it and out a small courtyard and past two more houses along an alley before they came to a house better than the others. It took only a few moments for the guard captain to vouch for Eugenio. The captain himself escorted Eugenio the rest of the way through the alley and down past another house before they knocked at the side door of the big hacienda where the colonel lived when he was in Taos.

"Nothing?" Colonel Sinfuegos bellowed when Eugenio finished telling about their assault on the train. "You brought back no gold at all?"

"*Nada*. It went well until some she-bitch came and turned it all around." Quickly Eugenio described the woman who had done so much harm to their cause that day.

For a moment Eugenio waited for a reaction from the colonel, fearing the worst. He looked up, surprised, when Colonel Sinfuegos chuckled.

"So, my young friend, you have met the White Squaw. I have heard of her often, seen her once or twice, but never had her anger directed toward me. Now I am afraid that we will be hearing more from her right here in Taos."

"How, Colonel? Why? She does not know who I am. We were well away from your retreat."

"Ah, but she will know. Who else in this wasteland would have the men and the affrontery to attack a federal gold coin shipment in a Railway Express car? Yes, she will come."

Antonio Sinfuegos leaned back in the cushioned chair and tore two grapes off a bunch that had been recently chilled. He ate them with relish, spitting the seeds on the floor.

"Oh, yes, she will come. You said a woman and two children died on the train. For that alone she will come. This White Squaw is also called Rebecca Caldwell. She is half Sioux Indian. She is twice the man most of those she faces are. She can shoot better than they can, ride better, endures the heat or cold better, and usually comes out on top in a showdown with outlaws, gunmen and lawmen alike.

"Yes. By now she has heard of me, has me figured as the power behind the attack, and she will come first hunting you, and then me. We shall handle her when she arrives. Your only job from now on is to kill her."

"Shoot a pretty woman?"

"Kill her any way you can, without warning, without mercy, without the hint of any sexual desire. Go now and prepare your rifle. It will be a better weapon than your *pistola*."

Eugenio's eyes widened. "Colonel, it is that important? She is such a threat? So dangerous?"

The small man with the deadly eyes looked at his lieutenant. "Eugenio, you have seen her in action. What would she do to my operation here if she were to be allowed to do as she wished?"

The skeletal-looking man blinked his dark eyes and slowly nodded.

"Yes, yes, I understand, my Colonel. It will be done."

Colonel Sinfuegos nodded, then reached in his small desk and took out a special stiletto. He held a thin strip of paper and sliced it in half.

"If you get close enough to the pretty one, use this. I need a new tobacco pouch. One of her breasts will make a fine pouch." The small man smiled, showing his teeth, and nodded. "If it is convenient for you after she is dead."

Eugenio nodded slowly. "Yes, yes, my Colonel. It will be my pleasure. Whatever you want will be done."

"One more small item, Eugenio." The colonel made a motion with his hand, and two large men came into the room. One carried a square block of wood which he placed on the colonel's desk.

The Buzzard motioned for Eugenio to come closer.

"You failed in your mission, Eugenio. For that there is a punishment—nothing severe, but some-

56

thing that will remind you for the rest of your life that no one fails *el Zopilote*."

One of the men took Eugenio's left hand, folded the three large fingers into a fist and pushed the small finger forward over the edge of the wooden block. Both men held Eugenio now so that he could not move.

El Zopilote, the Buzzard, took an eight-inch, heavy hunting knife from his desk.

"Do not fail me again, Eugenio. Make sure you kill the woman within four hours of her arrival in Taos."

As he finished speaking, he swung the heavy knife down hard. The razor-sharpened blade sliced through flesh and drove through the small bone, chopping the finger off between the first and second joints.

Eugenio's knees buckled, and he passed out. The men carried him from the room. One held a cloth over the stump of the little finger to stop the blood.

El Zopilote nodded as the men left. Yes. It was as good as done. This Indian half-breed squaw would not interfere in any of his plans again—ever!

Gray Squirrel went down the ladder into the *kiva* carefully. Last week he had fallen from a ladder, and he didn't want to do that in front of the members of the council or the relatives of Red Willow.

The ceremonial room here at Taos Pueblo was twenty feet long and half that wide. It had been constructed with stone walls that had been carefully chinked with smaller stones and then plastered over with adobe to form a smooth surface. The floor was covered with flat stones with mortar between them.

On the far end, a six-foot-wide platform had been built up a foot off the floor and again covered with flat stones that had been carefully set in place and mortared in solidly.

In the center of the *kiva*, a fire pit had been built. At

the other end of the room, a low masonry shelf had been made to hold sacred objects. Behind this shelf was a niche in the wall where masks were stored when not being used during certain festivals. The Pueblos called this niche the *kachina* house.

In the floor near the same end of the room was the *sipapu,* the most sacred part of the *kiva*. It was a cavity in the floor a foot deep and ten inches wide and covered by a piece of smoothed-out cottonwood plank. In the middle of it was a four-inch-square hole filled with a wooden plug. Sacred figures were often set around this plug. This was the symbolic representation of the place where the Pueblo people emerged to the surface of the earth, and a contact between the natural and the supernatural worlds.

The others had already assembled in the *kiva* when Gray Squirrel climbed down. He sat with the relatives on the platform. Red Willow's body lay on the floor near the cold fire pit.

Two Feathers began the prayer chant, pleading with the great spirit to accept Red Willow's spirit quickly, so that he would not be trapped on earth.

The sacred cornmeal was tossed to the four points of the compass so some of it fell on the body. There were more prayers, long ones that Two Feathers knew by heart. Then each of the survivors walked slowly past the body, sprinkling it with a pinch of the sacred cornmeal.

Next the dancers came and with their death masks in place danced around and around the body to help release the spirit. Two Feathers did a short dance, and the ceremony in the *kiva* was over. The masked dancers carried the litter holding the body up the ladder, and the procession moved to the plaza where the public part of the ritual of a fallen hero was conducted.

It too was brief, and the *kachina* dancers had a larger part. As the ceremony ended, the dancers still in their death masks led the way up the stream and into the canyon on a trip that would take them high on the crest of the mountain where Red Willow would be placed on a newly made burial platform.

There, in the open and as high on the mountain as practical so that he would be as close as possible to the great spirit, Red Willow's spirit would have a good chance to leave his body and fly to the place of the many spirits. He was tied securely on the platform so that animals could not carry off a part of his body.

Later his family would return to the mountain place, gather his bones and put them to rest in a burial ground that they had used for hundreds of years for the ordinary members of the clan.

Gray Squirrel and Two Feathers did not make the climb. It was for the family and the *kachina* dancers. The two elders of the tribe hurried back to the *kiva*. There was to be a council, and the wisest men in the pueblo would consider what action to take in response to the death.

The other members of the council were there, twelve of the wisest and most respected men in the pueblo. Quietly they heard the witnesses who saw the shooting relate exactly what happened.

Each man on the council who wished to would have the chance to speak about the death. There was no time limit and no order of procedure. Several of the men thought that a life for a life would be fair. Even the white men would understand this.

Who, then, would be the white man to die? The one who killed Red Willow, of course.

Gray Squirrel cleared his throat, and the others stopped talking and looked to him.

"The one who killed Red Willow is called Montrose; he is a chief among the whites. He has many horses and wagons and hauls in goods the whites use. Would it be fair to exchange Red Willow, a young

59

man yet without children, for a white chief?"

As they talked, a young man came in the *kiva* and spoke to Gray Squirrel. The talk had turned to other means of balancing out the laws of justice.

Gray Squirrel spoke again. "The white chief has brought to the widow of Red Willow a gift of six of the white man's buffalo, the long-horned steers, and a wagon loaded with twenty-five bushels of shelled, well-dried corn."

There was an immediate chatter among the council. Such a great gift had not ever been experienced by anyone in the pueblo.

"That is five times the corn that Red Willow and his woman could grow in a whole season," one of the council said.

"The white man's steers can be grazed and butchered when the woman of Red Willow needs the meat and hide," another said. "She is the richest widow in the pueblo."

"The woman of Red Willow is heavy with child. Would it be just for this white man, Montrose, to provide for the woman and her child until she takes a new husband?"

"It would be just," Two Feathers said softly.

"Would it be enough?" Gray Squirrel asked.

After another hour, the council had not decided if it would be enough. They left the problem hanging and sent for Hawk Caller. This young man had come to them from a pueblo to the south where he had studied the white man's tongue and had much English. He was instructed to seek out the man with the shiny star on his shirt and tell him of the decision of the council.

"Tell no one else, only the star man," Two Feathers instructed. "Then return here with any words that the star man might have for us."

Someone mentioned the knife fight in the white man's village.

60

"One man fighting with another man is no concern of the council," Gray Squirrel said.

When he learned that the young man was Red Willow's brother and that the Tewa was hunting for the man Montrose, Gray Squirrel sobered.

"Ask the young man to come to my rooms. I will talk with him. We have trouble enough with the whites. We do not want this to build into a conflict that can't be resolved by chiefs sitting down and talking it out."

Two Feathers rose and climbed the ladder out of the *kiva*. The council was over.

Rebecca Caldwell arrived in Taos on the Highland Stage at a little before six P.M. She had her heavy bag and was on her way to the only hotel. She had trailed *Šila* on a lead line behind the stage from Santa Fe, then had him put in the livery stable. Rebecca looked up when she heard gunshots. She put her bag next to the barbershop and investigated. Halfway down a stub alley, she found two men beating up an Indian.

One of the men held a gun as the other one pounded on the young Indian who looked to be about eighteen. Then they traded.

Rebecca drew one of her Smith and Wesson American .44's and slammed a round into the building over the men's heads.

"That's enough of that," she bellowed.

The two white men turned slowly, one with his hand near his holsters, the other letting the muzzle of his six-gun point down.

"Well now, what do we have here, a young boy or a woman dressed up like she wants to be a man?"

"Put your gun away and let the Indian go," Rebecca said as she kept walking toward them. She stopped thirty feet away.

"Holster that six-gun, now!" Rebecca barked.

The man with the weapon in hand laughed.

Rebecca shot him in the right shoulder, spilling the Colt from his fingers.

"Damnation, woman. What the hell you doing?" the wounded man screeched. "This is just an Injun. The damn Injuns stopped us working on the new warehouse, and we need the job. We're trying to talk some sense into at least one of these damn Pueblos."

She walked up, her weapon's muzzle dead centered on the second gunman.

"Ease that iron out of its home and drop it," Rebecca said.

"Not a chance. Go ahead, shoot me."

Rebecca walked closer, and when she was three feet away, she leaped forward and brought the barrel of the Smith American down in a slashing blow across the man's forehead. He screamed and dropped to his knees.

She had seen that the Indian had not moved during all of this. She holstered her weapon and used the plains Indians' universal sign language to tell the brave that she was a friend and that he was safe now.

He signed back his thanks, and turned to go. Only then did she see where he had been wounded in the leg. She called out sharply and stopped him, then picked up the two six-guns from the men on the ground and threw them on the roof of the closest building.

"Next time you want to fight with somebody, give me a call. I'll be pleased to keep it simple and make it fair. Or wouldn't you two like to try a fair fight?"

She turned her back on them and helped the Indian walk down the short way out of the alley. Once there, she stopped and used a kerchief to wrap up his leg wound. The bullet had gone on through and missed the bone. It wouldn't be serious. The young brave wore only a blanket tucked in around his waist and, she assumed, a breechclout. With his leg bound up, they continued, and she walked beside him.

She signed that she would see that he got safely back to his village. He nodded and motioned and led the way to the seven-storied pueblo.

Rebecca had been to Taos before, but not for several years. She asked about the old chief, Raging Buffalo, but learned that he was no longer with the clan. Their way of saying that he had died. A moment later from one of the high sets of rooms, a tall, gray-haired Indian came out and looked down. The brave she had brought back called to him, and the older man made his way painfully down to the lowest level of the pueblo.

When he was close enough for his old eyes to focus on her, he smiled.

"White Squaw," he said softly in English. Then he signed that he was Gray Squirrel and that he had heard of her. He was pleased to have her in the Taos Pueblo.

CHAPTER 6

Gray Squirrel invited Rebecca into a first-floor pueblo room. They went up the ladder to the roof and down another ladder into the living space. He explained how most families had three rooms, but more could be built if needed. When a young man married, he went to live with his wife's people; it was simply the way the Pueblos did things.

A shy Pueblo woman wearing a manta, a one-piece garment looped over the left shoulder and leaving the right shoulder and arm bare, brought cold water and cakes made of cornmeal. The cakes were good, and they ate and talked. They discovered they knew a few of the same words. The sign language the Pueblos used during market time in the fall worked well between Rebecca and the chief.

He told her about the problem with the sacred burial ground of the chief of chiefs', and Rebecca frowned.

"The land will be kept sacred," she signed to him. "I will not let the white men put up any building on that area. I'll talk to them tonight. There must be a way found so the white man can have a building, and so the grounds can be kept sacred."

Gray Squirrel told her about the brave who was shot to death and of the gift from the white man. She agreed that the white man must supply food and shelter for the woman until she remarried.

Gray Squirrel signed of the growing unrest among some of the younger Taos men who thought that the white men and the Mexicans were crowding out the Taos who had lived there for fifteen generations.

Rebecca nodded. She asked him by sign: "What do you know of the Mexican called the *Zopilote*, the Buzzard."

Gray Squirrel smiled, then signed. "We know of the name. We have heard he is a *bandido* with clean feet. He has never harmed our people or caused us any pain or suffering."

Clean feet. He apparently had not been arrested or charged with anything because it could not be proved.

Rebecca saw that it was getting dark out. She had to get to the hotel. She said good-bye to the old chief, and he told her to come anytime. She could live with the Taos Pueblo people if she wished.

"I might just do that later on, but now there are things I must do in the town."

"I will send one of my men to see you safely back to the white man's buildings," Gray Squirrel signed.

She walked quickly through the growing darkness, and never once heard the brave who followed her, but she knew he was there. When she came to the first buildings, she heard the call of a night hawk from behind her. Rebecca smiled and made a return cry of the same hawk, thanking the brave for guarding her. When she walked down to the barbershop where she had left her suitcase, she saw that the establishment was still open.

As she picked up her suitcase, the owner came out and nodded.

"Evening, miss. Saw you leave your bag. Figured I better stay open until you came back for it. Not that anyone in town would steal it."

"I'm beholden to you, sir. I came in on the stage. Is that the hotel down there?"

"'Deed it is, miss. I'm Ingemar Olson. Good to have you in town. I'll close my door and pull the shade and walk you on to the hotel. Just to be sure some drunken teamster doesn't forget his good manners."

"That's not necessary."

"'Deed it is, miss. Ain't seen such a pretty lady in town in an old mule deer's age, so I want to pay my respects."

"That's kind of you, Mr. Olson. I'm Rebecca Caldwell. Can you tell me where the sheriff's office is?"

He pointed it out to her as they walked. He carried her bag in to the desk at the Sangre de Cristo Hotel.

"Buford, you find this lady the best room in the place, y'hear. Whole town going to be mighty upset with you if'n you don't treat Miss Caldwell here like a genuine queen."

"Thank you, Mr. Olson."

He tipped his hat and smiled and then walked out the front door with a little skip to his step that hadn't been there all day.

Rebecca registered, took a room on the third floor, and then went to see if she could find the sheriff. Not one to waste a good opportunity, Rebecca had slept halfway up here on the stage, so she was well rested. She had remembered what stage rides were like, so she had bought a large soft pillow before she left Santa Fe. Nothing helped a stage ride so much as a soft pillow to put on the hard wooden seats to buffer some of the bounces, jolts and bumps.

Acting Sheriff Wonlander looked up as she came into his small office. One deputy was there, but Sheriff Wonlander stood and went to the wooden counter that separated the front of the office from the rear.

"Yes, miss?"

"Are you the sheriff in this county?" she asked.

"Yes, ma'am. Acting sheriff until the next election."

"Thought you might be able to help me. I'm hunting for a man who tried to rob a train outside of Santa Fe. This man is so thin-faced he looks almost like a skull. Extremely deep-set eyes, and he's Mexican."

"Why do you think he's in Taos if the robbery was down by Santa Fe?"

"This is where his boss lives. He works for a man I'm sure you've heard of, *el Zopilote*."

The lawman nodded. "Sure, heard of him. The Buzzard. Some say he works out of Santa Fe, some say Denver, some Salt Lake. He moves around a lot. What makes you think he's here in Taos?"

"Some friends of mine in the Federal Secret Service from that same train say that he lives here."

"If he does, what's your business with him?"

"Blood business. He killed four people on that train he tried to rob. His men did. He murdered a woman and her two small girls. Shot them down like they were bottles on a fence. And he killed a friend of mine."

"Yes. You seem upset by that."

"I watched them die. Now I want to return the favor to this skull head and his boss. Is he in Taos?"

"We hear stories. I have my suspicions. But what I need as a lawman is evidence. I don't have any; I don't know how to get any."

"What are your suspicions? Who is your suspect?"

"Sheriff's business, miss. I can't tell you that. He's a bit of a hero here in Taos—if this is the right man. The one I'm thinking of helps out widows, gives young men work, helps get medicine and pays doctor bills for the sick."

"He should; he steals the money from the *gringos* and robs trains."

"Proof, Miss Caldwell, what we need is proof. Best I can do for you."

Rebecca stared at him for a minute, then spun around and left. Most lawmen she got along with fine, but this one wasn't the most cooperative. So she'd have to go to the best gossip parlor in town, a saloon.

She picked out the fanciest one along a block of businesses and went in. She heard a pair of hoots as she walked to the bar, slammed a quarter down on the shiny surface and glared at the apron.

"I want a beer and none of your sass. I'm here for a drink and some conversation. Who the hell in this town knows what is going on?"

The barkeep drew her a draft beer, took the quarter and returned two silver dimes to her. He grinned. "Me, I know what's going on. What you interested in, politics, domestic disputes, outlaws, or who is trying to get whose wife into his bed?"

"Outlaws. *El Zopilote*. Is he in town now, who is he, and where can I find him?"

"You don't want much. Yeah, he's here. The sheriff's been trying to get some hard evidence on him for two years. He keeps his skirts clean in the county. Does his raiding and killing and all the illegal stuff well out of town."

"He has the local Mexican people on his side?"

"Damn well does. Feeds them if they get hungry. He can afford it."

"Does he have a guy work for him who is so skinny his face looks like a skeleton?"

The barkeep laughed. He was about thirty, with soft blond hair cut so short it stood straight up on top. He was tanned and fit-looking. Now he laughed again.

"Yeah, you described him to an eyelash. That would be *Polluelo;* the Mex word means chicken. He's a wild man, who does exactly as the Buzzard tells him. He's a bad man to get angry at you."

"So am I. Where can I find him?"

"There's a cantina about two blocks up. Just on the edge of the Mex town. I wouldn't go in there on a bet, so I wouldn't suggest that you try it."

"The Buzzard. He has another name?"

"Sure, Colonel Antonio Sinfuegos. Lives like a Mexican don and thinks of this town as his. He's king to the Mexicans, and about half the white men who run Taos, including the whole damn city council, don't want to cross swords with him."

She sipped at the beer. It was cold. *They must have ice here from somewhere,* she thought.

"What about the warehouse?"

"Yeah, some big dangerous mixup. This guy Montrose claims he has a deed to the land. City council looked into it, and the guy he bought it from didn't have any clear title at all. It was all made up out of whole cloth and a bribe to the county clerk, looks like."

"So no building on the burial grounds?"

"Looks like it. But the Indians are still in a snit about it. Now Montrose is furious that he lost the cash he paid for the corner lot, and he's looking for some land somewhere else. Course the Taos Injuns are mad as hell about their brave who got murdered on the holy land. One hell of a rhubarb."

"Okay, thanks." She held out her hand. "I might come by again and ask some more questions. My job is to know this town in a rush and find the man I'm hunting. My name is Rebecca."

They shook. She nodded, turned and eased her Smith and Wesson Americans in and out of the leather as she glared at the men in the saloon. Nobody said a word. She turned and walked out without a backward glance.

Rebecca got to the door, then slipped through it quickly into the shadows away from the glow of the

69

windows. Something wasn't right. She had felt it in the saloon, and now again out here. A small skittering of electric energy ran down her spine, and she looked both ways down the street. It was something she couldn't explain. A part of her Sioux heritage maybe, an instinct of survival, the Indian in her that gave her an advantage over a common white man.

The hotel was across the dirt avenue. One brightly lit saloon was between here and there. The yawning black hole of an alley sat beside a dark business across the street.

Was she getting jumpy? All her imagination? Hell no! She loosened both .44's and drew her right one, then walked quickly into the deeper shadows along the false front of the hardware store. Her boots made a racket on the boardwalk. She eased up, stepping silently on her toes until she was across the boards. There was a gap in buildings next to the hardware store, so there was no walkway there.

She had just stepped off the boards to the dirt when a flash of a gunshot blossomed from the alley across the street. A rifle! Almost at the same time she sensed more than saw movement in the gap between stores and spun and fired into the darkness a fraction of a second before a revolver flashed a shot at her. She pulled the trigger again, adjusting her sight to just over and to the left of the gunflash, and fired twice. She heard a wail of pain and the sound of running feet through the empty lot away from the street.

The rifle across the street spoke again, twice, and she felt a burning sensation across her left arm. Then she sprinted past the open space to the next store and dodged behind a freight wagon that had parked there for the night waiting to unload.

The rifleman was still there, but he had no shot now. She could wait him out. She had removed the threat behind her. The gunman in the gap between stores was wounded and gone. She could now make a dash for it across the street for the safety of the hotel.

Then she wouldn't know who was gunning for her. Two of them. They had followed her, set her up like a target in a shooting gallery. Only the darkness had saved her skin. She felt her left arm. Blood seeped through her shirt. It was just a graze from the rifle bullet. Too damn close.

Who knew she was in town? Why were they gunning for her? Her only thought was that *el Zopilote* was behind it. He must have had a report from someone who had been involved in the attempted robbery. But how could he identify her so quickly and spot her coming in on the stage?

Someone had. She made up her mind in the blink of one of her cobalt-blue eyes. She checked her loads in the revolvers, filled each with six rounds, and blasted two lead slugs into the alley. Then she rushed around the far end of the freight wagon and charged across the street. One round came from far behind her but was wide. A rifle boomed from the alley, but the hot lead didn't come close.

Rebecca surged to the boardwalk and slowed, stepping across it silently until she was against the clapboards of a store. Then she began to work without a sound toward the alley, hugging the storefront. The alley was next to the dry goods store, and she paused when she was ten feet from the black void.

She listened. Nothing. She paused and waited. Someone cleared his throat. Then she heard the lever work on a rifle. Rebecca edged closer, pulled both Smith Americans from leather and stepped silently toward the void.

She heard a tentative step in the alley; then the man cleared his throat again.

Now! She jolted around the corner of the store and fired three times with each of the guns, bracketing and blanketing the twelve-foot black space of the alley.

71

Without a wasted effort, Rebecca darted back behind the safety of the storefront.

As the blasting of the six rounds faded down the alley, she heard doors slam and windows open. A voice screeched about trying to get some sleep. A saloon half a block down gushed a dozen men into the street staring her way and yelling questions.

Down the other way she heard a voice she recognized, the sheriff bellowing something unkind.

She listened to the alley. For a moment all was quiet; then a low groan came and a shuffling of feet. Rebecca leaned around the corner and fired once more in the direction of the sound.

"Hold it!" she barked. "You move again and you get ten rounds in your belly. Stop right there and live."

A six-gun barked as she again pulled back from the alley. Then she pushed both Smith Americans around the wooden corner and blasted the last three rounds from her twin revolvers.

The groan came louder; then the voice rose into a scream, and she heard the sound of a man falling hard to the dirt in the alley. Then all was quiet.

A rough hand grabbed her shoulder from behind. "What the hell, a woman?" Someone ran up with a coal oil lantern. The sheriff scowled. "So it's you, Caldwell. You been in town two hours and already you shoot up the place?"

"Two of them shot at me first, Sheriff. One across the street and a rifleman in the alley. I think this one is still here."

The sheriff took the lantern, and they walked into the alley. About fifteen feet in along the near wall they found him. He was a Mexican with a long moustache. A rifle lay beside him, and a six-gun was still in his hand. He had three bullet holes in his chest and one in his left leg.

The sheriff sniffed the rifle and the pistol. Both

had been fired.

The lantern light washed over the dead man's face. Rebecca saw that he was not the Chicken.

"Who is this man, Sheriff? Who did he work for?"

"Yeah, I've seen him. We've had trouble with him before. He was one of the best Mexican shooters in town. Who did he work for? No question there. He was one of *Zopilote*'s top guns."

"The Buzzard. So it was him. How did he know so quickly that I was here?"

"The Buzzard has ears everywhere. Everything that happens in Taos and in the pueblo gets to him within minutes. By now he also knows what hotel you're in, what room and how good you are with those hoglegs."

The sheriff paused for a moment. "You best come down to the office and write out a statement. I'd hate to have you turn up dead before morning so I couldn't get my paperwork. Around here, some things can't wait until daylight."

CHAPTER 7

In her third-floor room that first night in Taos, Rebecca Caldwell pushed the dresser over to block most of the window, then put a straight-backed chair under the door handle so it rested with only two feet on the floor. If anyone broke in from the door, they would make so much racket half the hotel would hear them. If someone tried to come down a rope and get in the window, he would find the way blocked.

She put one of the .44's next to her pillow and slept like a newborn.

The next morning she talked with the sheriff again. The family had claimed the body of the man who attacked her in the alley. The colonel had come to the office to launch a protest and urge the sheriff to find the murderer at once.

The sheriff told Colonel Sinfuegos that the man had been in a shootout with another person, and it had been declared by witnesses to be a fair fight. The case was closed.

Rebecca had kept to her working clothes, clean, long-sleeved white blouse to cover up her wounded arm and a pair of brown pants along with her brace of .44's. She stopped by the doctor's office, Dr. Vince Madden, but he said that no one had been in over the night or that morning with a bullet wound. She showed him her arm, and he clucked a moment, then put some of the new antiseptic on it, watching to see if she reacted to the burning sensation. When she didn't, he smiled and added some salve, then bandaged it lightly with a white cloth. Her blouse sleeve covered it completely.

"Should be fine in two weeks. You were lucky it wasn't deeper, or a foot to the right."

"You're right. Doctor, do you report to the sheriff any bullet wounds you treat?"

"Of course."

"Good, remember that applies to Mexicans and Indians as well as to whites."

The doctor gave her a strange look as she flipped him a silver dollar and went out the door.

She spent the rest of the morning getting to know the little town again and walked as close to the big house of Colonel Sinfuegos as she could without bringing out interested Mexican men who could only be guards.

In the afternoon she found the builder at the lumberyard. Webb Bryce was candid, pleasant and, she thought, interested in her as a woman. She kept the talk on a business level.

"So you thought you had a legitimate contract to put up the building, and you checked for ownership at the county courthouse."

"You bet. I thought it strange that the area right beside the ruins of the old pueblo would be private land. The Taos Pueblo got a Mexican Land Grant that evidently holds up in our courts. So they own a good-sized piece of property. But this was right on the edge of it, so I figured it must be all right."

"I understand you're on the city council as well, Mr. Bryce."

"That's right. We do what we can for Taos."

"I'm sure you do. But right now doesn't there seem to be a lot of unrest? The three teamsters who were

75

killed. That's still unsolved. The murder of the Indian man at the burial grounds. The knife fight, to say nothing of the two men who tried to gun me down last night just after dark."

"You don't say!"

"I just did. You've got a regular hailstorm of crime going on. Do you think the Indians will go on the war path over the burial grounds?"

"Oh, Lord, I hope not. We've got troubles enough. These teamsters come rolling into town and think they own the place. We have more trouble with them than anyone."

"Even than with *el Zopilote?*"

Bryce looked up quickly. "How do you know about him?"

"Secret Service agents of the U.S. government told me about him. I'd heard of him before. Now he's settled down here in Taos. Nice that the local lawman and the city council look the other way when he raids and kills and shoots down women and children."

"That's not true, Miss Caldwell. We just don't have any proof we can take into court."

"Sometimes with men like the Buzzard, the court of the *pistola solamente* is the best kind."

Bryce looked puzzled for a moment. Then he frowned. "The pistol, the gun, the . . . single gun. That would be illegal and immoral, Miss Caldwell. Certainly the city could never justify anything like that."

"But you sit here and let him send his men out to rob and plunder and murder. Mr. Bryce, I was on a train three days ago, and I saw one of this Sinfuegos' gunmen shoot down a woman and her two small daughters. He murdered them in cold blood like they were nothing more than targets for his amusement. I don't care how it's done, Mister City Councilman, but that man is going to be stopped even if I have to

76

do it myself using the court of the *pistola solamente*."
She turned and walked out of the office and through the lumberyard to the street.

When she came to the corner where the chief of chiefs' burial ground lay, she stared in amazement. A crowd of more than fifty people was milling around. Then she saw why. There were a dozen Taos Indians standing in a rough line near the inside edge of the burial grounds where they met the old pueblo ruins.

Each of the men had half of his face painted black, and each held a rifle. Half a black face. That meant the Pueblo Indians were half ready to go to war.

Well in front of them lay the ruins of the burial platform that had been built. The travel tipi had been smashed down, and the buffalo-leather covering had been slashed and ruined. Three of the circles of stones around burial plots had been kicked aside and mixed.

As she watched, Gray Squirrel, wearing his white blanket and now a headdress with twenty eagle feathers in it, stepped out of the ruined pueblo and walked in front of the line of warriors. With him came a smaller, young Indian who understood enough English that he could interpret. He had done this before for Gray Squirrel.

The Pueblo chief stopped ten feet in front of the Indians with the rifles. He stared at the people and then spoke. The tone was harsh and demanding. Hawk Caller repeated the words in English but without the anger.

"Where is your chief?"

Acting Sheriff Wonlander hurried up, but Gray Squirrel waved him aside and spoke again.

"Your town chief must come, not your star man. Where is your town chief?"

Webb Bryce came out of the crowd and walked to the edge of the sacred land. He did not step on it.

"Tell Chief Gray Squirrel I am the town chief, Chairman of the Taos City Council. We don't have

77

a mayor."

When Gray Squirrel heard the translation, he nodded, then walked forward but stopped so that he remained on the Indian land.

Hawk Caller translated quickly as Gray Squirrel spoke.

"Your white men have wounded us. You have violated our holy and sacred burial ground. You have smashed our burial platform and ruined our tipi. Two of our young men in the tipi were beaten and chased away. Your whites are acting like the bull elk who eats the loco weed and goes crazy.

"A white man has killed one of our braves on this sacred land. He must be punished. We have decided that a life for a life is fair. The white chief must die."

Owen Johnson, one of the city councilmen and a lawyer, eased up near Bryce. He had heard the translation as had about half the people there, and there was a murmur of anger through the crowd.

"Careful what you say," Johnson cautioned him. "Stall him, say we have laws that must be followed. Try to make him happy, but put off any decision."

Bryce nodded at the lawyer and looked at Gray Squirrel.

"We grieve for your slain brave. It was a white man who tasted the fire water and went crazy even as the bull elk does with the loco weed. He has taken stores of food to the widow. He will help support her until she finds a new husband.

"This . . . this vandal work here is what young boys do who are not real men. They are children and do foolish things. The white man's council has agreed that the land where you now stand is sacred to the Taos Pueblo, and must remain with your people. Perhaps a stone fence around it would help protect and identify it as part of the Pueblo lands."

All of this was translated a line at a time by Hawk Caller. When the talk was done, Gray Squirrel shook his head.

"The council of the Taos Pueblo has spoken. After this last violation of our sacred lands, we now demand a life for a life. The Pueblo council says that the chief called Montrose must be dealt with for murder by the white man laws. He must die, even as he killed Red Willow. The council of the Taos Pueblo has given the white chief three days to carry out this matter of justice."

Without waiting for any response, Gray Squirrel turned and marched back to the line of warriors who held their rifles. Gray Squirrel vanished into the ruins of the old pueblo, but the ominous line of Indian riflemen remained where it was, guarding the sacred land.

Bryce took a deep breath and turned to the assembled whites.

"Now, just settle down and let the council deal with this. I've instructed the sheriff to strictly enforce a new law we passed this morning. No white person or Mexican is to step so much as one foot on the Indian lands they call the sacred burial ground. As soon as possible we will construct a wooden fence two feet this side of the burial grounds to wall the white folks away from the sacred lands.

"Until then, I want all of you to stay away from the Indians. Don't do anything to get them any more riled up than they are right now."

Acting Sheriff Wonlander came up with three deputies and motioned for the people to move back from the Indian burial land. They moved but still did not quite understand.

"What's so blamed sacred about a bunch of old bones?" one man asked.

"Don't matter," the deputy nearest him said. "Law says we stay off and away from it, so that's damn well what you do or get your ass thrown into jail for seven days. Oh, yeah, on this one, if you're in jail, you provide your own food, or you don't eat."

Rebecca smiled when she heard how Bryce had handled the situation. Still, he had an explosive problem on his hands. There was no law in this state making it a crime to kill an Indian. So what could the city council do? The sheriff couldn't even arrest Montrose. But if the town didn't at least put him in jail, the Indians would most likely kill him themselves.

Whatever happened, she would have another long talk with Gray Squirrel before the three days were up. Perhaps something could be done to cool down the Indians.

She looked up and saw the stagecoach coming into town. It was early today, not yet five in the afternoon. She watched it wheel past, then she headed down the boardwalk toward the stage office. There might be a package there for her. The Secret Service man said he would send her all of the written material they had on *el Zopilote.*

She came to the station just as the last passenger stepped down from the big rig. The driver took a large envelope out of the box under the high seat and read the front of it.

"Anybody here named Rebecca Caldwell?" he called out.

Rebecca stepped forward and held out her hand. "That's me, Rebecca," she said.

The driver eyed her a moment. "How I know you're the right one?" he asked.

"She's Rebecca Caldwell, Amos, I can vouch for her," Webb Bryce said from just behind her. The driver shrugged and gave her the envelope. Rebecca turned toward Bryce to thank him, but he was shaking hands with a tall well-built man about thirty-five years old, Rebecca estimated. When he turned, he smiled at her, and she felt an instant jolt as if someone had stroked her arm.

He was over six feet tall, with sturdy shoulders

under a suede jacket, and wore a wide-brimmed brown hat. He had on a string tie over a white shirt, brown pants and hand-tooled cowboy boots. He easily was the most handsome man she had seen this side of Arizona.

The moment vanished as he looked back at Webb Bryce, and the pair walked down the street. Rebecca walked carefully over to the side of the stage office building and leaned there a minute. Her breath came in quick gasps as she realized that she had been holding her breath. That was ridiculous. No man could affect her that way.

She took several more deep breaths as she watched Webb walk the newcomer down the boardwalk. Webb carried the man's sleek, leather suitcase.

Then they were gone in a mix of people coming and going from the stores.

Rebecca tried one more deep breath, then remembered the package in her hand. She looked at it and saw her name, with Taos for an address, and the initials of USSS in the upper left-hand corner.

Eagerly she opened the large brown envelope and looked at a dozen sheets of paper. Most were filled with writing. One was a drawing, and another a print of an old photograph. She pushed them back inside the envelope and walked down the street. She'd go to her hotel and devour this information about the Buzzard, before she figured out any detailed plans. It was evident that he had good security around his stronghold. Just how to get through it could be a problem.

On the way to her hotel, she passed the sheriff's office, and she looked in. Webb Bryce had his back to her, but it was obvious he was introducing the newcomer to Sheriff Wonlander. She wondered who the stranger was and, more to the point, why Bryce had met him at the stage and taken him directly to the sheriff's office.

Probably none of her business. She had her mind set on getting to her hotel to read what the Secret Service knew and thought they knew about the Buzzard. She had just entered the hotel lobby when she remembered that she had been running around so fast that she had forgotten about any midday meal.

She smelled the food from the dining room and automatically turned that direction. The reading material, no matter how interesting, would have to wait.

The only table left was set for three, but the waiter led her there and seated her. She studied the limited menu, a choice of prime rib or chicken. She was about to decide on the chicken, when someone walked up and stopped near the table. She looked up and saw Webb Bryce and his new friend.

"Miss Caldwell, would we be imposing on you to share your table? There would be quite a wait for another one, and we're in a bit of a rush tonight. Poor Ned hasn't eaten a good meal since he left Santa Fe this morning. You know that stagecoach meal service."

She looked at the stranger. He was the man from the stage.

"Oh, pardon me," Webb said quickly. "My manners. Miss Rebecca Caldwell, may I present Ned Silver, from Denver. He's here on business." Ned Silver stepped forward and took her offered hand, but instead of shaking it, he caught it by the fingers, turned it and brought it up to his lips, where he kissed it softly.

"Miss Caldwell, I've heard that name somewhere before. It would be a big favor to share your table, and of course I'll be honored to have you as my dinner guest."

It all happened so quickly she could do little more than nod at them. Rebecca was sure that she wouldn't be able to say a word if she tried to open her mouth.

82

Up close he was gorgeous, even better than her first evaluation. His smile was beautiful, showing even, white teeth as he gazed at her with his light green eyes. Dark hair tumbled down on his forehead, and he had an efficient, almost animallike way of moving.

At last she found her voice.

"Mr. Silver, Webb. I'd be delighted to share my table with you." She sought Ned Silver's eyes and locked on to them with her gaze, and his smile broadened.

"Fine, fine, Miss Caldwell. You've seen the menu; what would you recommend?"

They all decided on large slabs of prime rib, and the table talk soon switched to business.

Webb looked at Rebecca. "You might as well be the first to know. Ned Silver has come to town to be our newly appointed acting sheriff. Deputy Wonlander is now his captain and reports to Ned. This is something that's been coming for some time, and we finally did it. We just figured we needed some professional help."

The name had been pounding at her brain ever since she heard it. The term "gunman" rushed to the front, but that wasn't exactly right. She had heard the name a dozen times in the past few years. Always concerning some particular spot or town. Then she had it.

Rebecca smiled and looked over at Ned. "Well, it's good that when Taos was in trouble they went for the best in the business. Now I've made the connection, Ned Silver, town tamer! Welcome to Taos."

CHAPTER 8

The supper was an outstanding success. Rebecca thoroughly enjoyed herself, and she was aware that she was talking fast and bubbling like a school girl. Bryce gave her an odd look once or twice, then gave up and told Ned Silver that he had a room here at the Sangre de Christo Hotel.

"I'm sure you can find the way, Ned. I'll see you in your office tomorrow morning at eight, and we'll start laying down some of the rules and regulations we want you to start enforcing."

They had just finished small dishes of ice cream. It was the first for the territory and the hotel had made a big splash about serving ice cream free with each full dinner ordered. Ice cream had quickly become Rebecca's favorite dessert.

Ned waved good-bye to Bryce and then stared at Rebecca.

"Now I remember where I've heard your name. Rebecca Caldwell, the White Squaw. The lady who battles anyone who tries to take advantage of whites or Indians alike."

He watched her closely. "Yes, I can see the Oglala Sioux in you. You carry it proudly, like a banner, a guidon."

"I am proud of my heritage. Now I hope I can be of

some help to the Pueblos here."

Ned Silver chuckled. "I hear that you're much more interested in the Mexican situation, one *el Zopilote*, to be exact.

Her smile faded, and a grim resolve replaced it quickly. "That's right. Do you have any problem with that?"

"Absolutely none. Perhaps we can work together on this situation."

Her smile blossomed. "I was hoping that we could. But first could we explore some close cooperation in another area?"

"I'd be glad to. What?"

"Could you find room thirty-three in half an hour?"

His grin broadened, and he nodded. "Yes, I think I could do that. All I have to do is check in."

"Make it a third-floor room." She stood and watched him rise quickly. "I'll see you then." It was barely a whisper, but he heard; and Ned Silver smiled as she turned and left. He finished his second cup of coffee, then paid the check and moved to the front desk and found his bag already in a second-floor room. He changed it to the third floor.

"It gets me up and away from the heat of the street," he told the room clerk.

Precisely thirty minutes from the parting with Rebecca, he knocked on her door at room thirty-three.

It opened at once as if she had been waiting for him. She had braided her hair down each side with thick strands dropping just behind each ear. She wore a beaded headband with one white and black eagle feather in back. From the sides of the headband, small leather strips ended in a profusion of soft yellow feathers gathered in a ball.

She held out her arms so that he could see the white elk-hide dress she wore with a dozen beaded story pictures on it. Her moccasins were of white doeskin, cut low as the Sioux wore them.

"Like I said, Mr. Silver, I am proud of my Indian heritage. I like to wear these clothes when I deal with my Indian friends."

"Beautiful," he said. He closed the door gently. She walked toward him, put her arms around his neck and drew his face down to kiss him.

It was a long, steamy embrace that soon found Rebecca pressed tightly against Ned Silver. The kiss ended, and both were breathing heavily.

"Dear Ned, I am a direct person. If I like a man, I let him know as quickly as I can. If I want him, I show him that too as plainly as I know how. I'm no stranger to men. I was a Sioux warrior's wife when I was fourteen years old. I married two Sioux braves and bore one a child who I saw slaughtered in a raid by the Crow.

"I know more about lovemaking and how to satisfy my man than most women, and right now I want you to get out of those fancy clothes."

She met his lips again and pushed her hands through his shirt to massage his hairy chest. His own hands worked between their bodies and closed around one of her breasts which he kneaded and petted softly through the delicate elk-hide dress.

He bent and picked her up and carried her across the room to the bed. She had thrown down the light blanket, leaving the sheets, and now she spread herself on them languidly, lifting her knees so that the while elk dress slithered down her legs to her waist. She wore nothing under the dress.

"Now," she said, reaching for his fly, tearing at the buttons, feeling his turgid manhood continue to rise. "Yes, yes, Ned, right now, before you undress."

She pulled his lance from the restricting cloth and fondled it with both hands, then lifted and kissed the throbbing organ. She spread her legs wide and pulled him over her, and he lowered and gently felt the well-spring of her lusty nature.

Rebecca moaned softly, her eyes wide open searching for him, her lips parted until his mouth found hers and his tongue drove inside her mouth. She whimpered in the total joy of it and caught his buttocks and pulled him downward toward her secret place.

For a moment she writhed on the sheets in wonderful expectation, then stilled and caught his throbbing organ and directed it down and down until it met her body and he lanced through the lacy petals of her flower.

"Oh, glory!" Rebecca whispered. "Glory, glory. Deeper, drive into me with all of it. So wonderful!"

Rebecca gasped in delight, her breath whistling in and out now as her hips began a gentle rotation and an easy thrusting upward to meet him.

She caught his face between her hands and drew it down to kiss, then watched him. "How can it be so thrilling?"

"You, Rebecca, are the thrilling part. So slim and sleek, so fantastic, enjoying sex and making it tremendous for me as well."

Then they were gasping too hard to talk, and a moment later they both exploded and blew into dozens of pieces and rained down on the bed somehow gluing themselves back together.

Later they lay in each other's arms, resting.

"To think that I almost didn't take this job," Ned whispered.

"If you hadn't, I would have hated you for the rest of my life." Rebecca sat up and kissed him. Then she lifted the white elk-hide dress over her head, making the braids bounce and the feather balls fly.

Ned sat up now as well, feasting with his eyes on her slender, bronzed body with apple-sized breasts slightly upthrust with firm, bright pink nipples. His hand reached out and caught a breast, fondling it, then twirling the nipple between his finger and thumb.

"So beautiful and so feisty. Is it true that you tracked down and shot most of the old Jake Tulley Bitter Creek gang and your two uncles?"

"True. The bastards sold my mother and me into slavery to the Sioux just so they could save their worthless hides. I was with the Sioux four years. My mother lost her mind and died in the Indian camp. I could kill the Tulley gang ten times over and never repay them for what they did to my mother."

"What about what they did to you?"

"I was young; I could adjust. For a while I thought I was all Oglala Sioux. Iron Calf, my father, at last told me I was half Sioux, and for a while I was so proud I hardly thought about the outside. I adapted. My mother fought them and went insane and died."

"You survived and have become a force in the West. Hardly a lawman in the Far West doesn't know of you."

"Some of them hate me."

"They don't know you. I want to know you again, right now."

He did, and for the next five hours they made love and rested and talked and planned. It was nearly three in the morning when they at last fell asleep in each other's arms.

Colonel Antonio Sinfuegos wore his military uniform this morning. It carried the badges and insignia as well as the colors of the Mexican army, but he never showed it outside of his compound. He sat at his breakfast table sipping grape juice and eating thin slices of an orange with powdered sugar on them. He had the oranges brought in specially from Santa Fe from the fruit vendors.

"I am surrounded totally by idiots!" he bellowed. "Is there no one here who can kill this White Squaw? Where have all of the real men gone? What are you all, a bunch of old women and crones dreaming about the men they had fifty years ago?"

He ate another slice of the orange. "Has it come to the point where I must do my own work? Eugenio shot twice and whimpering like a kicked cur huddled in his bed. I lose five more men on the train. Bastards!

"Now I find that Raymundo has been shot four times in the chest by this *puta* of a White Squaw and even now waits for his burial." The colonel ate another orange slice, savoring the tartness of the fruit against the mellowness of the powdered sugar. Delicious.

"Very well. Let any among you who can do the job, do it. I'll pay two hundred dollars in *gringo* gold coins for the head of that bitch Rebecca Caldwell. Her head in a bucket. This time I want to be sure she is *muerto*."

The colonel waved one hand, and the forty men who had sat listening to him in the open courtyard below stood and slowly filed out the doors from the open square and hurried to their houses nearby.

Most of the men found their revolvers and rifles, cleaned and oiled them, and then one by one drifted out of the compound and through Mex town toward the place where the *gringa* lived. Each man had dreams of what he could do with two hundred dollars in gold. Few of them saw more than ten dollars of cash money a year.

Rebecca was gone from her room when Ned Silver woke up that morning. He swore softly, checked his pocket watch and saw that it was only a little after seven. He would have time to shave and dress and eat

89

some breakfast before the eight o'clock takeover of the county sheriff's office.

He smiled as he remembered the previous night. It had been delightful, and he had every right to think that this was only the beginning.

For a moment he compared Rebecca with the small blond lady he had taken to the opera in Denver only a few days ago. He guffawed at the contrast. He would never even say hello to that blond lady again. He was spoiled by the feisty, sexy, beautiful lady Sioux, and he loved it.

The five men who had come with him on the stage were at the office when he got there. The county had seven deputies, a lot for the area. He put them in one room and talked to them.

"There are going to be some big changes around here, deputies. The seven of you will carry out your normal duties. Me and my five men won't interfere or disturb you in the least. We will be a special force. It will be our job to be sure that every citizen and guest in Taos County hues to the line as laid down by our laws.

"My special deputies, or 'regulators' if you prefer, will be strict, tough, firm, maybe rough at times, but they will see that the laws are upheld. We probably will need more jail space. I'll arrange for that at the ice house and perhaps at a warehouse or two. Any questions?"

"Sir, do we report to you or to Sheriff Wonlander?"

"You still report to Captain Wonlander or anyone he designates. For the next thirty days I am the appointed sheriff of this county. Captain Wonlander will take over again when I leave. For you it's business as usual. Of course, we'll want to be sure that you stay out of the way and don't contradict any order or actions by one of my men."

After the meeting with the deputies had concluded, Ned entered the sheriff's private office, where his

90

man, Larry Hodge, had a list of laws they would enforce.

"Looks like lots of these been on the books here for twenty or thirty years and just forgotten. Just what we need."

Silver looked over the list. He checked off fifteen of them. "Have the printer run off fifty handbills with these fifteen laws and post them on every store in town and any spares on the trees. As of tomorrow at sunset, all of these laws will be strictly enforced. The first one on the list is that no one may carry a firearm within the city limits of Taos, except those duly sworn in as county deputy sheriffs or town marshalls of this city."

Ned chuckled. "The city fathers are going to have a ruptured spleen about some of these. I better make sure that we have a written contract before these hit the streets."

An hour later, he came out of Owen Johnson's office with a signed contract in his pocket. He was to be the master of this small city for a period of thirty days, and no one could fire him, rescind the contract or discharge him for any reason whatsoever.

Ned Silver chuckled and hurried back to the hotel dining room, hoping that he might find Rebecca having an early noontime meal. She wasn't there.

Rebecca had taken *Šila* out for an early morning run. The big Appaloosa had been corral bound for three days, and he wasn't happy. She ran him for two miles, then walked him back up the gentle slope. He recovered well and let her know he appreciated the romp.

About a quarter of a mile from town, she came upon two young white boys on horseback practicing roping a stump from their mounts. But as she came closer, she saw that it wasn't a stump they were practicing on. They had tied a young Mexican to a stub of a sapling and were casting at him with their lariats.

She rode up and bumped into one of the youth's horses and snatched the reins from him. Her angry scowl frightened the fourteen-year-old as much as her words.

"What are you doing to that poor boy?"

"Just practicing. Ain't hurting him none."

The other youth rode up. "You let loose of him. We ain't doing nothing wrong."

Rebecca drew her right-hand .44 and checked it so quickly the two young riders' mouths gaped open in wonder. "So, if you aren't hurting anything or anyone, I suggest that both of you take turns being tied to the stake." She motioned to the boy on the farthest horse. "You first."

The young man, who she figured was maybe fifteen, shook his head.

"You want to see how far you can ride before I shoot you out of the saddle?" Rebecca asked.

"You . . . you wouldn't do that. You're one of us."

"Not true, I am one half Oglala Sioux Indian."

She let that sink in. She had put away the elk-hide dress and wore pants and a brown shirt, but still had her hair braided on each side. The headband and the feather balls were gone as well.

She motioned with the Smith and Wesson American at the closest rider. "You, get down and go over there and untie him, and bring him back here."

The youth watched her .44 warily, slid off his horse, ran to the sapling and untied the Mexican while whispering to him. Together they walked back to the horses.

"Did they hurt you?" Rebecca asked.

The Mexican lad shook his head.

"Did you let them tie you up or did they make you stand there."

"They make Juan stay at stake."

"What should we do with them, Juan?"

"Whip them!"

"Would that make up for how they treated you?"

"Si!"

"Well then, boys, you better both take off your shirts and bend over and grab your ankles. Have you ever seen a person whipped?"

Both youths shook their heads.

"So, strip off your shirts."

The whites looked at each other, then scowled and unbuttoned their light shirts and threw them on the ground. Rebecca moved slowly forward, caught the reins of the second horse and motioned to the Mexican. He ran toward town. She led the horses and rode at a gallop away from the two white youths behind her. When she caught up with the Mexican, she took his hand and boosted him onto one of the horses, and they rode together at a walk toward town.

The dark-eyed youth looked at her several times.

"You really half Indian?" he asked in almost perfect English.

"Yes, Oglala Sioux."

"They call you the White Squaw?"

She turned to the young man. "Juan, how would you know that?"

"It is all over our town. The colonel call in many men and tell them to find you and to shoot you. He say he wants your head in a basket and he will pay any *hombre* two hundred dollars in gold."

They rode another few paces, and she watched him.

"Juan, why do you tell me this?"

"Because you helped me."

"The boys were just playing. It was a cruel game, but they wouldn't have hurt you."

"Hurt plenty!" Juan said. He showed her a rope burn around one side of his neck.

They rode a few more minutes; then Juan looked at her again. "I do not want them to hurt you. I will tell them what you did for me."

Rebecca smiled at the boy. "Thanks, Juan. But it wouldn't make any difference. The colonel is the one I have to talk to. He is the problem."

She motioned for him to get down. "Tie the horses beside the trail. The boys will find them as they walk back to town. You want to ride behind me the rest of the way?"

Juan shook his head as he watched her.

"I will tell everyone what you did. It might help." He ran up the trail, cut into the brush along the creek and was soon lost to view.

Rebecca smiled as she rode the rest of the way into town to the livery. She was glad now that she had trailed *Šila* on a long lead behind the stagecoach from Santa Fe. She had paid the driver ten dollars to take it easy on the trip, and *Šila* had made it with no problems. It had been a bit hard on him, but she had reassured the big Appaloosa at every stop that he was doing fine.

She had arranged for the driver to stable *Šila* as soon as they got to town. A five-dollar gold piece had sealed the deal.

She rode back to the stable and brushed down *Šila*, then poured grain into the stall feed box and hurried out. As she worked, she watched everyone in the livery. There was one Mexican, but he was busy cleaning out the stalls.

She would be alert for all Mexicans now. There was a price on her head, and it was enough to fire up the whole Mexican town. Perhaps she would have to do some of her work at night.

She had to find Ned Silver and tell him about this new threat. He might have some ideas. Also she was interested in seeing a town tamer at work. At work taking a town, that is. She knew how well he worked in bed, and she hoped there would be a lot more nights to experiment.

94

CHAPTER 9

Rebecca didn't take any chances. She left the livery and went to the first alley and from there down one alley after another until she came to the back door of the jail in the small county courthouse.

A lot seemed to be going on, but when Ned saw her, he left the three men he had been speaking with and came over to her.

"The word is out on the street that you're a marked target," Ned said, anger and a touch of caution tingeing his words.

Rebecca nodded grimly. "To think that I'm only worth two hundred dollars. That's an insult. A lousy bank robber gets a wanted poster for five thousand sometimes." She grinned. "Nobody's got my head in a bucket yet. I've got sources on the street as well."

"You want to stay here in the jail for a few days to let things cool down?"

"Absolutely not. I'd rather go after the Buzzard tonight. He'll probably figure this head money will get me into action. So I'll fool him. I can afford to wait. How is my favorite town tamer?"

"Hate those words. I'm just a man who enforces the laws. Look at the ones we'll be enforcing starting tomorrow at six P.M."

He handed her a list. She read it quickly and

looked up. "You're joking. No guns in town, no saloons open after eight P.M. Those two right there are enough to close down the town."

"It's the law. Take the city council a week to change the laws. Maybe by then we'll have something to show for our efforts."

She frowned. "Like what?"

"We'll run some of the scum and riffraff out of town. We'll try to pull the fangs out of *el Zopilote;* maybe we'll even come up with a solution to the three-day deadline for getting Montrose dead or turned over to the Indians."

"That's a tough one. I'm going to go out and talk to Gray Squirrel about it."

"You can talk to him?"

She made some signing to him, but he stared at her blankly. "I sign with him, the universal language of the plains Indians. Most of the people in the tribes can talk to each other that way."

"Be damned. Heard about it but never really saw anyone do it."

"So this is what a town tamer does, enforces the laws on the books and generally stirs up everything."

"About right. Then the good people of the town get off their duffs and come forward and establish workable laws, taking some responsibility for local government, and the town gets back on stride again."

"But usually you don't have three separate societies to deal with."

"Right. Here it's really only two, since the Pueblo lands are outside the city limits."

"But the Pueblos are going to have a lot to do with how things go here," Rebecca said. "Like that three-day deadline."

"That worries me. Not much I can do about it. That's up to the city council." He chuckled. "They saw the posters already and are as mad as hell. They

96

told me I can't do that. I showed them the laws on the books and told them they can change the laws; but by their own charter it takes two readings of any change of a law, and the two readings must be before public meetings and at least seven days apart."

"They hired you; can't they fire you?"

"Not with the iron-clad contract I have. I saw to that. This has happened before."

She touched his shoulder and smiled. "You busy tonight?" she asked softly.

"Not that busy. My room, thirty-one, that way if you have any late-night visitors. . . ."

"Good idea. Oh, do you like wine?"

"Yes."

"Good, we'll have some wine and cheese and crackers tonight, to keep up our strength." She grinned and headed for the back door.

"Rebecca, you want me to assign a man to you? I've got some good ones."

"I can take care of myself. If I can't, I shouldn't be doing what I'm doing. These guys are amateurs."

"Hey, pretty lady. It doesn't matter how smart or how good the finger is that pulls the trigger. That damn chunk of lead does the same job when it hits somebody."

"Fine, I'll be sure it isn't me." She winked at Ned Silver, slipped out the back door to the jail and checked both ways, then she walked down the alley with her right hand at her side, near the butt of one of the Smith and Wesson American .44's.

They had moved the city council meeting to the back room at the Jackstraw Saloon three doors down from the Taos bank. All five of the members were there. Lynn Keating had come straight from the range and still had on his blue jeans and sweat-stained plaid shirt.

97

"We've got two more days to get something done about Maxwell Montrose and his Indian threat," Webb Bryce said. "Just what the hell is it going to be?"

Owen Johnson shook his head. "It's a dilemma. We can't legally arrest Montrose for anything other than firing his weapon in the city limits, which is a misdemeanor with a ten-dollar fine. I'm afraid that wouldn't satisfy Gray Squirrel."

"Those Indian guards still standing on the burial grounds?" Ingemar Olson, the barber, asked.

"Were when I came in," Josh Randall said. "They look like they intend on staying there for as long as it takes."

"The idea of a wall around the damn burial grounds is a good idea," Ingemar Olson said. "Then we won't get caught tromping on their ancestors. But what the hell we going to do about their ultimatum on Montrose?"

"We could talk Montrose into leaving town," the rancher said. "Say he went away for six months; the damn Pueblos gonna forget all about it by the time he comes back."

"Good idea," Webb said. "I'll suggest that to him this afternoon. Any other ideas? Where are we legally?" He looked at Johnson.

The lawyer shook his head. "We don't have a hand in it at all. Someday there will be laws against killing Indians. But right now we can't charge Montrose, so we can't arrest or try him. What it comes down to is that it's between Montrose and the whole damn Pueblo tribe."

"That doesn't give Montrose much of a chance."

"We need the man here in town to run the freighters," Randall said. "They're a wild bunch at best, and he's just wild enough to keep them in line."

"Is there any chance he could buy off the Pueblos?" Olson asked. "Say he agreed to provide the tribe with five head of cattle a month. What would that do for their tribal life? They wouldn't have to trade for buffalo meat and bones and sinew. They could postpone their usually unproductive hunting trips for deer and elk. They would have a continuing supply of meat."

"Yeah, but five steers a month!" the rancher snorted. "Damn, that's gonna cost him two hundred dollars a month. Good steer is worth forty dollars at the railhead."

"Might beat selling out and moving," Webb said.

"Or running out of town and then having to sell out," the lawyer added.

"Worth a try," Webb said. "Is it agreed?" He looked around and saw the other four nod. "Good, I'll get in touch with Montrose and talk to him. I'll have a meeting with him today, and then this afternoon try to get a talk with old Gray Squirrel."

"What if Montrose won't agree?" lawyer Johnson asked.

"Hell, then he'll have to run. No other way unless he wants to decorate a Pueblo room with his scalp lock. Oh, they'll kill him good enough, but they'll give him a chance. Ten warriors with bows and arrows and Montrose running his ass off down some canyon. Not much of a contest."

Webb cleared his throat and waved at the men. "Let's move on to another problem. Have you seen the flyers that are going up on the streets this afternoon?"

"Damn right, and I don't like it," Randall said.

"Best way in the world to close up a town, take away the guns and the booze," Keating blurted.

Webb held up his hands. "All right, to some extent I agree. But we hired him to clean house. We knew these laws were on the books. I for one didn't know he was going to enforce them."

"We can always fire him, send him back to

Denver," the barber said.

"Not a chance," Johnson countered. "We signed a contract, remember? You approved it. He's got the job for thirty days, and there is no way, not a chance, not a possibility, that we can fire or replace him. He saw to that in the wording. He even gave me some of the language he assured me had been used before in contracts like this one."

"So we got fucked good," Randall said.

"Not necessarily," Webb countered. "Some of the old laws might do the job here. Let's see how it goes for a few days. We can always get the ones we don't like off the books after a week and two readings. It's all in our charter."

"Still don't like it," Olson said.

"Hell, Ingemar, I'll buy a couple of bottles and you can come over to my house after work and get drunk as a skunk." They all laughed. Ingemar wasn't a drinker.

Webb got their attention. "As I remember, the fines are set on most of these fifteen laws Ned Silver is going to enforce strictly at ten dollars, or ten days, or expulsion from the town. That's what we wanted in the first place: to get rid of some of the drunks and deadbeats around town, especially in the saloons."

"Yeah, but will it clean out Mex town?" Keating asked. "Far as I'm concerned, the damn Mexicans should stay below the border, unless they want to learn to speak English and to rope a cow."

They all laughed. "Yeah, Keating, but you're a wild-eyed radical. Everybody knows that." Johnson said it. There was a look that passed between them the others didn't catch.

"This better work," Josh Randall said. "Otherwise we're going to have a mighty slow month around Taos."

The meeting broke up then, and Webb Bryce headed down the street toward the freight line. He stepped into the office of Inter-Mountain Freight

Lines and found the owner in his private hideaway spot upstairs over the storage.

Webb went over the proposal with Montrose and then settled down in a chair and eyed the freight man.

"Don't see you have much choice, Montrose. You try this buy-off idea and see if it works. If it does, you buy the steers from Keating and drive them up to the pueblo monthly. Maybe Keating will give you a cut-rate price of thirty dollars. That's still a hundred and fifty dollars a month."

"Hell, usually I don't clear that much a month," Montrose said. He stood and paced around the small upstairs office. "Not that much business up here. In the winter when the trail gets clogged, I'm snowed in here except for a light sled rig or two, and they won't haul much."

Montrose stared at the wall, his red face even redder now. "Christ, I have a choice of going broke, or selling out and running away day after tomorrow, or getting roasted over a fire by the damn Pueblos."

"That's about it," Webb said. "The only alternative would be to start your own cattle ranch."

Montrose felt his anger surge and swore. "Go ahead, dammit! Talk to the goddamn chief and see if he'll go along with the five steers a month. No, first offer him three steers a month. He might go for that.

"I'll wait and see what he says. Otherwise, I'm on my horse and riding out of here. Tell Owen Johnson if I'm gone to hire somebody to run the place for me. Damn, this three-steer deal has got to work."

Webb patted the man on the shoulder as he left. Montrose had dug a big hole for himself. Now it was up to the whole town to try to get him out of it. If worse came to worst, the county could help pay for the beef. It was partly the county's fault that the building had been started.

If it hadn't been for that fake first grant deed on the property sworn to and filed with the county clerk, no construction would ever have been started on that burial ground, and there would be no problem today.

Webb took the trail up to the pueblo. He saw no guards, no sentries. At least it wasn't on a war basis yet. Those Indians with their faces painted half black had scared him yesterday. That was what they did when they went to war, only then they painted the whole face.

He came to the edge of the pueblo and asked for Gray Squirrel. Webb was actually near the plaza. Someone ran to find Hawk Caller. He was nearby and came soon to talk to the town chief, Webb.

"I need to see Chief Gray Squirrel," Webb said.

"What will you talk with him about?" Hawk Caller asked. "The chief will ask me the purpose of your visit."

"Tell him I want to talk about Montrose. We have a solution to the problem."

Hawk Caller nodded and hurried away. He entered one of the second-floor houses, and Webb leaned against a low platform and waited.

After five minutes, Gray Squirrel came from the closest set of buildings and walked to where Webb waited.

Hawk Caller was there to translate.

"Chief Gray Squirrel, I come with good news. We have found a way to solve the problem of Mr. Montrose."

The old chief looked up, but Webb could read nothing from his face.

"Nothing can be gained by another death. Innocent people would suffer even as Red Willow's widow suffers. If Montrose were to die, no one would be left to bring her beef. What we suggest is that the man Montrose be required to bring three beef cattle to your pueblo each month for two years."

He stopped and watched the old Indian as Hawk Caller translated. There was a momentary flicker of his glance toward Webb, but no other reaction.

When the translation was finished, Webb waited.

Gray Squirrel squinted at the midday sun.

"White Town Chief, would the three steers a month bring back Red Willow? Would the three steers a month make Red Willow's wife and soon-to-be-born child miss their dead man any less? Would the three steers a month bring to a halt the Pueblos' mourning the loss of a fine young man?"

"No, Gray Squirrel, but three beef a month would show that the white eyes know of your loss and sympathize with you. They would show that the white village is in harmony with the pueblo and enjoys the Mother Sun when she rises in the morning and understands that the earth is forever with us and can be made to do our will and grow our crops."

When the translation was finished, Gray Squirrel nodded. "You are wise for being so young. The winters have not yet given you snow hair, but you speak with wisdom and honor.

"We the people of the Pueblo Taos speak with one tongue. The white chief, Montrose who killed Red Willow, must die. If your laws do not require that a murderer die, then give Montrose to the pueblo, where the laws are just and swift, and the killer of a young man will die to pay for the great evil he has done."

"There is no other way?"

"There is no other way. The one called Montrose must die." Gray Squirrel watched Webb as the translation was made, then he turned abruptly and showed his back to the white chief as he walked back to the first row of the pueblo houses and climbed the ladder to the roof.

When Webb could see the chief no longer, he turned and walked back to the village. What now? he wondered. He had to tell Montrose first, then he would talk with the council again. They only had a day and a half left to come up with a solution.

103

CHAPTER 10

El Zopilote paced his third-floor study. The plan was almost finished. Yes! He would dynamite the Santa Fe railroad tracks in the mountains due east of Taos. It would be a downgrade just beyond a curve so the engineer would have no time to stop.

The train would crash, and the Railway Express car would spin off the tracks and hurtle down some canyon. Only then would he and twenty-five men sweep out of the timbered slopes and attack the train. They would blow open the express car, then blast apart the safe and anything else that might hold the just minted United States gold double eagle coins coming from Denver. This particular train would carry more than one hundred thousand dollars in coins headed for Texas, Louisiana and the deep south destined for banks. He would have it all!

This might be his last raid. He would have more than enough gold and currency by then and could slip across the border and buy a small village somewhere and live like a king for the rest of his life. Oh, there would be the *federales* to pay, but they were always there. A few *gringo* dollars a month would satisfy them.

Yes, yes!

He paced to the window and saw another of his

men leave the compound and filter into the street. The *hombre* had a heavy revolver on his hip.

Good! The men were working at their job. Soon now, very soon, the White Squaw would be no more. It would be impossible for her to escape the forty guns that were searching for her. He was only surprised that it was taking so long.

He looked at the map again of New Mexico. It wasn't complete, but showed the string of peaks of the Sangre de Cristo Mountains between Taos and the valley where the iron horse charged north to Denver.

They would not strike blindly across the rough country. There was a trail of sorts that went across the mountains and wound past Eagle Nest Lake. Yes, the route was well known. He could put twenty-five men on the train and come away with a hundred thousand dollars.

He had to remember that so many coins were heavy, an ounce each, sixteen to a pound. He took a pencil and paper and did some figuring. That would be 6,250 pounds of gold! He would need pack mules. At two hundred pounds per mule it would take thirty-two mules. Yes, it would be done. First he had to find the pack horses or mules, either one.

He would lead this attack himself. Any trainmen or passengers who survived the crash would be no problem. He would kill any who got in his way. No mercy, no quarter, the gold or else!

There was just one irritant he had to deal with here in Taos first, the White Squaw. That would be done quickly. This new man in town, Ned Silver, shouldn't be any problem. He was a lawman, enforcing the old laws on the books. Yes, no guns after tomorrow at six and no saloons open after eight P.M. He didn't stand a chance of enforcing those laws.

It might be amusing to watch. If it did work, if the people put away their guns and the town tamed down, Antonio Sinfuegos knew that he might have to consider taking over the whole town, wiping out the lawmen and holding the town by force.

He could raise almost a hundred gunmen for such a takeover. He doubted if there were fifty whites in town who could shoot. Yes, it would be a battle, but one that he would win. In Taos' Mexican town, loyalty to him and his system came first among the Mexicans.

The Indians would not be concerned. It was not their town, and the pueblo would not be touched.

The colonel sat back in his favorite chair and motioned with his hand. At once Conchita came into the room. She wore a thin blouse and a skirt that came off easily. He knew she wore nothing under the long dark skirt.

She smiled at him and stood next to his chair. He pulled her down on his lap, and she yelped in delight and kissed him on the cheek. Slowly, gently he lifted the thin blouse off her arms and over her head. His eyes glittered at her big, naked and delightful *tetas*. He bent and kissed one, then the other, and Conchita sighed and worked her hands inside his shirt to stroke his chest.

Antonio Sinfuegos growled deep in his throat and picked up the slender girl and carried her across the room to a sofa. Conchita was fourteen and delicious. It would be an enjoyable afternoon. By then, for sure he would hear that one of his men had a bucket with a head in it to show him. Yes, it was going to be a good day all around!

When she left the sheriff's office, Rebecca had walked down the alley to the back door of a small restaurant where she had eaten before. The cook waved at her and looked out at the counter and six tables. A Mexican man sat at one of the tables with his back to the wall drinking a cup of coffee. His right hand stayed near a holster on his hip.

The owner of the cafe, a big, heavy woman with sagging breasts and an always smiling face, saw Rebecca and went to her.

"Heard about the head money. You don't want to eat at the counter. How about I fix you something in my little office over here."

"That would be kind of you."

"Hey, us girls got to stick together. No bastard gonna shoot you full of holes in my place."

Rebecca held out her hand. "I'm Rebecca Caldwell."

"Yeah, everybody in town knows you, Rebecca. They call me June, 'cause that's my name. How about a big bowl of beef stew? I cooked up a potful last night and this morning."

Rebecca ate the stew with relish, along with two big slabs of fresh-baked bread and some currant jelly and two cups of coffee.

June looked in and nodded. "I love a good eater. You stay here awhile if you want. Must be every Mex in town is gunning for you. What the hell did you do?"

Rebecca grinned. "Nothing yet. It's that old Buzzard who is afraid of what I'm going to do. The man is right. I've got my sights set on him, and he won't last another week."

June nodded. "Damn I love a woman with some guts. Only thing is I don't want you spread out all over town because of some damn Mexican with a double-barreled shotgun."

"Won't happen. I'm doing a lot of alley walking these days. Right now I'm heading for the pueblo. I can hit it if I keep to this alley out back of you and go north, can't I?"

"Right," June said, staring at Rebecca. "Yeah, I guess I do see some of your Sioux pappy in you.

Makes a right pretty picture, Rebecca Caldwell. You come back for supper; it's on the house. Be my little celebration that you're still alive."

"That's a deal," Rebecca said. June refused when the White Squaw tried to pay her for the dinner.

"You take it easy. Most of them damn Mexes can't hit the ground with three shots. Even so, be careful."

Rebecca waved and headed out the door, checked the alley and, when she saw it was empty, walked quickly to the north. Her right hand stayed near the .44 as she moved.

At the first street, she checked both ways and trotted across the dirt throughway, then paused in the alley and looked around. She saw three Mexicans, but they were heading the other way.

Thirty feet into the alley, she checked behind her and saw the same three Mexicans run into the alley mouth. It was solidly built with stores on both sides the whole length. None of the stores or shops had an unlocked back door. She walked faster, then looked ahead. Two men came into the other end of the alley and stood waiting for her.

A damn trap, and she had stumbled into it. They probably had every alley in town covered by now. Two to one was better than three to one, so she drew both the Smith and Wesson .44's and walked forward until she was twenty yards from the two men. Now she saw that both had handguns out. At least they weren't shotguns.

She held the big .44's in front of her and began to run. When she was fifty feet away, she saw the two Mexicans begin firing. She waited another six steps, then at about thirty-five feet she fired with both .44's as fast as she could.

Her first barrage knocked down one of the Mexicans, so she concentrated on the other one, slamming three rounds into his chest before he could get his weapon reloaded. She put two more slugs into the first man to fall as she ran between the two and holstered her weapons and walked calmly out the other end of the alley. She turned and peered back a moment before continuing across the street.

Half a dozen men and women ran to the alley and looked at the two dead men. She slipped into the mouth of the alley across the street and hurried down it into the shadows. She met no one else in the next block, then she was out of Taos and moving up the trail by the stream toward the pueblo.

She paused halfway there and watched her back trail. No one had followed her. Rebecca hurried on to the plaza and met a woman carrying a basket of shelled corn.

"Where is Gray Squirrel," Rebecca signed. The woman shook her head indicating she didn't know the signing. She hurried away. A short time later a Pueblo man looked down from the roof of one of the houses.

She signed the same thing, and he nodded and motioned for her to come up the ladder. A few minutes later she sat in a room on the top of the five-story pueblo pyramid and looked out over the winding stream. Gray Squirrel had greeted her warmly and now offered her some cool water from the stream and some venison jerky.

"It is good to see you again," the chief signed.

"It is good to be here. Was it a good corn crop this season?"

"Better than last, not as good as some times."

They sat there smiling at each other, glad to have the required preliminaries out of the way.

"The white eyes are worried about your life-for-a-life decision about Montrose."

Gray Squirrel moved to ease the pain in his legs. "The white eye took a life; he must give us his life."

"You have heard of the Cherokee. They have a finely developed sense of justice. They do not believe

109

in an eye for an eye. They say a second death will not bring back the murdered man. Why not let the killer be punished every day of his life and not with death?

"They say let the killer be responsible for the wife and family of the dead man. He will hunt for them; he will protect them; he will pay money for them to survive. In this way the sense of justice is satisfied, and the killer will not suffer merely a few instants of his own death, but will suffer for years making payments for his vile act.

"The widow and her children will be cared for, and there will be one less death for some other friend or relative to grow angry about and come and try to settle with another life-for-a-life trade."

Gray Squirrel took a long drink from the pure cold water. He touched his lips.

"White Squaw, we know you to be *Sinaskawin* of the Red Top Lodge Oglala Sioux and a much decorated warrior woman. We know that you speak with the tongue of a warrior with much white-eye learning and much Oglala training and much warrior experience in both camps.

"We understand that the Cherokee are an advanced society, that they are keepers of the land and growers such as we are. But we are not as developed as they are in our understanding of the great spirits and their purpose for us on this Mother Earth.

"We can only do what we know and believe. Most of us are a simple people who believe in right and wrong, and when someone, especially an outsider, wrongs one of ours, we know only to demand an equal fate for him: an eye for an eye, an arm for an arm, a life for a life."

The signing took some time, and when Gray Squirrel finished, he looked at her for her understanding.

"I understand. The Pueblo people are strong in many ways, but the white eyes are stronger in some

110

ways. It would not be good for this one death to spark a war between the white eyes in Taos and the Pueblos. They are many. They would call in five hundred horse soldiers with the long knives and rifles that shoot many times and cannon that can smash a pueblo house with one large exploding shell."

Neither spoke for a moment.

"I do not threaten the Pueblo," Rebecca continued. "I speak as friend and half Oglala Sioux. There must be great council on this problem. Is there any way that the council of the Pueblo would consider anything less than the life of Montrose, the white chief?"

"We had considered it, *Sinaskawin*. That was before the infidels struck down our sacred platform and ruined the tipi and scattered and desecrated our burial land after they knew what it was. Before then we had considered such a Cherokee solution.

"Then came the insult to our ancestors, and our hearts were hardened. Now there is no way to undo what the whites have done. No way for the Pueblo to back down from a life for a life."

"It is sad. I am torn into two pieces."

Gray Squirrel reached out and touched her shoulder. "We understand, but what must be, must be." He watched her a moment, then moved and sipped the water signifying a new topic. "We hear that White Squaw is hunted in the street by the Mexican men with guns like she is a doe in the forest."

"This is true, Gray Squirrel. However, as you see, I am unharmed. They are boys against a warrior woman of the Oglala, so have no fear for me."

"You are free to stay with us. No Mexican ever comes here. They fear our spirits, say we are possessed. We have shelter and food and drink for you here."

She looked and saw some of the same household

111

items she had known as a Sioux. For just a moment it felt like home. She smiled.

"I would be pleased to stay here until sister night eats up the brother daylight. Then I must get back to the white-eye town. There is much for me yet to do."

She stayed, wandering around the plaza, visiting in several of the houses, looking out from the fifth-floor house at the surrounding countryside. She sat near the stream for a while, then dangled her feet in it and remembered how the Oglala children had splashed and hooted and screeched as they played naked in the creeks near the summer camps of her lodge.

She shared a meal of beans and cornmeal cakes and roast beef from the first of the steers that Red Willow's widow had butchered and passed around before it spoiled. Half of the meat she had cut into thin slices and hung on pointed hooks on a square rack so that the meat would dry in the sun. It would take three days for the beef to dry enough so that it would keep all winter.

She had given the hooves to the council and the bladder to a friend and the stomach sacks to others. The sinew from along the spinal column she had stretched and dried, and she would use it for sewing.

When the sun slipped behind the far ridges, Rebecca said good-bye to Gray Squirrel and several new friends and went back to town. There was much to do, but she wasn't sure where to start. She had become so wrapped up in the Montrose affair that she had, for a moment, lost sight of her main purpose here.

First she had to stay alive. She hurried down the trail and then watched the first buildings of Taos for several minutes. She saw a man in the shadows near the second building. She skirted the trail into town and went down a block to the next street.

Here she could find no one waiting for her. She

112

thought of going to the sheriff's office, but Ned Silver probably wouldn't be there. They were to be together tonight as they had arranged, but there had been no time set.

She slipped down the street to the side door of the hotel. A man came from the shadows, and she tensed. Then she saw the bottle he carried in a paper sack. He stumbled past her and continued down the alley.

Inside the hotel, she saw that the hallway was clear. She hurried up the steps and checked the second floor. No one lurked there. She found the third floor vacant as well and walked quickly down to room thirty-one.

She almost knocked, then tried the knob. It was unlocked. She stood at the side of the door and pushed it open. The room was dark inside. "Ned, it's Rebecca." She heard the click of a revolver hammer uncocking and the hammer being let down easily.

"Good, come on in." It sounded like Ned's voice. She hesitated a second, then stepped inside and closed the door.

A match flared in the room, and she saw the outline of a man's back. Then the lamp wick caught, and the chimney was put in place. When the man turned around, he wasn't Ned Silver.

He was a small Mexican man immaculately dressed in a black pinstripe suit and stiff white collar and fancy tie. His eyes glittered as he watched her. One hand held the lamp, and the other held a revolver cocked and aimed at her heart.

"Well, well, Miss Rebecca Caldwell, I presume. May I introduce myself. I am Colonel Antonio Sinfuegos. I hear you call me the Buzzard."

CHAPTER 11

Ned Silver paced the small sheriff's office. Twice he looked at his gold pocket watch. Two minutes until eight. It was dark outside, had been for maybe an hour. Where was Rebecca?

He hadn't seen her since she had visited him at the jail. He'd seen dozens of Mexicans on the street, all with revolvers, many without holsters. They were walking around looking for Rebecca.

So where was she?

If the Mexicans were still out there hunting, that meant that none of them had found her. He had sent a man up to her room in the hotel, but it was dark and empty.

Where did that leave him?

All afternoon since the posters had gone up, there had been a flood of people in the office screaming and yelling. Most of them were mad as hell about the new laws. He told them they were old laws and they would have to talk to the city council about that. They yelled some more and finally left.

Only the Baptist minister and the Catholic priest had said anything good about the enforcement.

What should he do about Rebecca?

Where could she have gone? To the pueblo? A possibility, but she would have told him. Would she stay there all night? Not likely when they had arranged to meet in his room tonight. Maybe she had gone there and was waiting for him. He looked around the new office, put some papers back in order on the desk and grabbed his hat.

He'd check his hotel room and then start making a round of the saloons and the street to see what he could find out. The Mexicans should know if she had been caught by the Buzzard.

Captain Wonlander stopped him on the way out.

"Oh, Sheriff, we've got the ice house cleaned out and ready. We can put maybe twenty men in there with two guards. Then, if we need it, we can use that old dry goods store down on Main. We can put maybe fifty in there, but don't think it's going to come to that.

"We make a big show arresting the first dozen or so, and the word is gonna get around town fast that we mean business. A working man don't like to spend a day in jail."

"Good, Captain. We'll talk about that tomorrow. We have until six o'clock tomorrow, right?"

Ned waved and slipped out the back door and headed down the alley toward the hotel. He got there in five minutes and checked for a light in his room. He thought his was the third window over from the end on the top floor. There was a light up there, but now he didn't remember if his was the second or third room. He hurried inside and started up the stairs.

Rebecca knew who the small man was the moment she saw him in the glow of the coal oil lamp. By then it was too late. Her six-guns were of no help, not with that big muzzle almost in her stomach.

"So this is what the bastard looks like who slaughters women and children in cold blood," she barked at him. "You're worse than I expected. You're vomit,

115

Colonel. You're slime. I can't think of words vile enough to describe what you are really like."

The slanderous outpouring hit Sinfuegos like a bucketful of cold water. His smile vanished, and he edged back a step, his eyes glowing cold and deadly, his breath coming in gasps. No one had ever talked to him that way! His finger tightened on the trigger.

"What's the matter, asshole? Too used to hiring other filth to do your killing? Too lazy and stupid even to pull a trigger? I should have guessed. Damn I'm tired. Put away that silly gun before it goes off and you shoot yourself in the crotch."

She pushed the six-gun aside and took three steps to the bed and sat down on it.

"Damn, but I'm tired. Well, big man, what are you waiting for? I hear you always rape women before you kill them. Figures. Hell, I couldn't care less. I've done men twice as good as you are, so I won't even feel that little finger you call your prick." Rebecca unbuttoned her blouse and pulled it from the pants and in one swift move shucked it off her arms and shoulders. She slipped the chemise over her head and sat there bare to the waist.

Sinfuegos stared at her, his mouth open, his glance frozen on her breasts. She shook her shoulders, making her twin peaks bounce and jiggle. Then she dropped her chemise off the bed near her right boot. The silk garment hit the floor.

"Oh, damn, it'll get dirty down there." She bent to pick it up and made her breasts bounce again. As she reached down beside her leg on the side where he couldn't see, she slid a stiletto out of her boot sheath and held it out of sight behind her leg as she stood.

"Well, what are you waiting for, Colonel? Am I more woman than you're used to?" She said it with a whine and a tease in her voice and took three slow steps toward him, pushing her breasts out at him, mincing up to him with a little swagger. Her right

116

hand kept the stiletto out of sight behind her leg.

Sinfuegos still pointed the six-gun at her. He swallowed and looked from her breasts up to her face and then down again, his mouth open, his breathing fast now. A line of spittle came out of his mouth and ran down his chin.

In a move so fast the bandit chief almost missed it entirely, Rebecca sprang the last three feet to the small Mexican man. The stiletto came up and slashed down across his wrist holding the six-gun, cutting deeply into the back of his right hand, bringing a scream of pain from him.

The weapon slipped from Sinfuegos' fingers as the colonel grabbed his hand and stared at her in total disbelief. By that time, Rebecca had raised the knife again and slashed at his face. The razor-sharp tip of the blade caught his left cheek and sliced a two-inch gash there before breaking free of his flesh.

Sinfuegos spun around bellowing in pain and fury. Before she could draw one of her six-guns, the bandit darted to the door and out it. He rushed down the hall as two slugs from Rebecca's left-hand American slid past his charging body. Then he was down the stairs and out of sight.

Rebecca started to chase him, but got only a step into the hallway when she realized she needed more clothes. She stepped back into the room as two doors down the way opened. There was a moment there when she had almost chased him shirt or no shirt.

She heard footsteps on the stairs and waited. Maybe he was coming back. Instead, by the hall lamp, she saw Ned Silver leaping up the steps three at a time and thundering down the corridor to the room.

He stopped when he saw her look out the door.

"Hey! You're here."

"True. Did you see my guest rushing down the stairs?"

"The small Mexican with a bleeding cheek and hand?"

"The same. Know who he was?"

"Some Mexican who tried to collect your head, I'd guess."

"Close. That was Colonel Antonio Sinfuegos himself. He was waiting for me when I came here to your room to see you. His voice even sounded like yours."

She stepped back and let him in the room, and he grinned when he saw her naked to the waist. She bent and picked up a revolver off the floor.

"This was what he greeted me with. I used some subtle arguments to talk him into not killing me."

"You also sliced his hand and face open with your knife and then ran him out of the room," Ned said. "Neatly done." He frowned. "The fact of the matter is he almost killed you tonight. Which means we can't stay here. Get dressed; we have to get out of here while we still can. He could have thirty guns outside in ten minutes."

She dressed, and they blew out the light and went into the hall. Ned checked the downward stairs and waved her forward. They got to the second floor, and he went to the lobby. There she heard a shouting match, and as it rose in intensity, she knew Ned's voice was one of them.

He was covering for her to get down the stairs and out the side door. She hurried down and saw Ned with his six-gun drawn backing up four Mexican men in the lobby. Rebecca slipped around the edge of the lobby and rushed out the side door.

She ran across the street and stood in deep shadows, one of the .44 Americans in her hand as she waited.

It was almost five minutes before Ned came out the side door. He looked up and down the street. She gave a morning dove call, and he sauntered across the street.

"Four Mexicans waiting to greet you. I lined them up and took their guns away on the pretext that they were not U.S. citizens and therefore not permitted to carry firearms. That's not true of course, but it worked. Come on."

He walked with her away from Main Street, down another block and then north fifty more feet to a small house.

"I rented it this afternoon. It was going to be a surprise for you. You should be safe enough here, as long as nobody sees you come or go."

Inside, it was small and cozy, furnished and stocked with food in the kitchen. The bed had even been turned down, and there was wood for the fireplace.

"No reaction, no letdown?" he asked.

"What do you mean?"

"In this business, I've seen strong men go through a fire fight or an arrest or any kind of violence and when it was over collapse in a heap. Some men cry. Some swear and drink. Some turn within themselves and won't speak a word. A simple mental reaction to the physical and mental violence."

"It never bothers me."

"Some crazy Mexican had a gun in your belly about to pull the trigger tonight, and you strip off your clothes to distract him, get a knife from somewhere and slash his wrist so that he drops the gun, and then cut him in the face and chase him down the hall—and you have no reaction?"

"Only one."

"Good, that's a start."

"I wish I'd killed him."

Ned Silver chuckled, then he laughed, and at last he hugged her tightly as he roared with a gut-booming release of his own. His eyes watered, and he slashed away the wetness, then kissed her gently on the lips.

119

"Damn but you are good, Caldwell. Damn good."

With no more talk, they locked the front and back doors, made sure the windows were closed and then went to the bedroom. He placed her on the bed, took off her boots, saw the stiletto, then pulled off her pants and slowly unbuttoned her shirt.

He kissed her, and she surged against him, holding him so tightly that he almost cried out. Then he smiled. Maybe this was her form of reaction and release.

She held him a long time, then let go and kissed him again and began to undress him. She started talking with no urging from him.

"You're right. I am reacting. I figured I was dead back there. He had me dead center, his revolver not two feet from my heart. All he had to do was pull the trigger. So I called him every dirty name I could think of. I accused him of slaughtering women and children, of being the most base and terrible person in the world. I think I shocked him so much that he *couldn't* pull the trigger. Then I chided him because he couldn't even kill a woman. I pushed the gun aside and sat on the bed.

"The strip tease caught him of guard again, and he was panting before I got my chemise off. That's when I figured I had him."

She kissed Ned again and rolled on her back on the soft feather bed. "Tonight I want to be all bare, and I want you as naked as I am. I want to make love until we don't have the strength to sit up. The kind of work we do, we never can tell when it will be our last time making love."

He caught her breasts and fondled them, caressed them, making them warm, and soon her nipples stood tall and proud. He trailed kisses around her breasts until she moaned with desire.

"You are so fine, so good. You know just what to do to make me go wild." Her breathing came fast now, and she writhed on the bed as his kisses moved down over her flat belly to the tangle of black hair over her secret place.

Her hands found his pants and pulled them off, then his short underwear and his shirt. She caught his lance and held it tenderly, then stroked it until he moaned and moved over her.

Their joining was better this time than ever before, soft, gentle, with whispered words of tenderness.

Then they both felt the surge of their bodies, and they raced to climb the hill, both peaking at almost the same instant as they bounced and pounded and drove deeply until the explosions came and they gasped for breath and died for a minute before they held each other and rested.

After ten minutes, he moved and she held him.

"Ned, how can it get better and better? One of these times we're going to reach such heights that we'll die in each other's arms from the pure ecstasy of it."

"What a wonderful way to go!"

She hit him on the shoulder.

At midnight, they got up and had fried eggs and grated potatoes fried in bacon drippings. They both were starved by that time and cleaned up their plates.

"You planned this, you scamp," she said. "You had food brought over and everything."

"Nothing is too good for the woman of my dreams."

She kissed him, and they left the dishes on the table and hurried back to bed.

"Just how long can you hold out?" she asked.

"Until three o'clock," Ned said with a grin.

She pushed him down on the bed. "Then, let's not waste any more time."

They didn't.

CHAPTER 12

When Rebecca woke up the next morning, Ned Silver had breakfast ready for her: two eggs over easy, toast, coffee and a big bowl of oatmeal and raisins with milk and sugar.

"My mother always figured a body needed a good start in the day after being starved all night," Ned told her.

Rebecca nodded, digging into the food with a good appetite. He watched her eat, and only then did she realize that he wasn't eating as well.

"Had my breakfast as I figured out what I was going to do today. The city council has called me to a meeting at nine. I figure that they want me to back down on the enforcement of the laws. Sometimes in these situations, the council members will have some special laws they want enforced, or some special people they want run out of town."

"But you don't work that way," she said.

"Never have, never will. When I get done with my thirty-day stay, the place will be clean and running like a railroad watch."

"No exceptions?"

"Not unless a majority of the ordinary people, the citizens, talk to me and show me that a gang of thieves hired me in the first place and my being there is making it easier for the bad guys to rob the county

122

blind and put the town out of business permanently. Happened once up in Idaho."

"What did you do?"

"Took six months. We had a recall election, threw the bums out, got the city back on its feet and put two of the bad guys in the state prison for ten years."

He watched her a minute. "You're almost as beautiful dressed as you are naked."

She looked up quickly. "I like you lots better buck-assed bare than I do with your clothes on. You have time?"

He chuckled and shook his head. "It's getting toward eight-thirty. You slept in. But I'm going to be available tonight. What are you going to be up to today?"

"Sinfuegos is the target. The problem is when he has forty or fifty men out hunting me, it's harder to get to him. I should have nailed him last night. Now I have to come up with a plan to get into his fortress and dig him out."

"I might have some ideas after my big battle with the city council."

"They doing anything about Montrose? I had a long talk yesterday afternoon with Gray Squirrel. He's solid as a rock on the life-for-a-life ultimatum. His people would have compromised before those jackasses defiled the burial ground the second time. Now he says that the hearts of his people have hardened."

"Don't blame him. In lots of states and territories the laws of the land apply to everyone, Indians included. New Mexico will get around to giving the Indians dual citizenship sooner or later."

"So you have no problem with the idea that Montrose should die for killing the Indian?"

"None whatsoever. He made a mistake. If the Indian had been a white man, Montrose would probably have been tried and hung by now. We'll just have to wait and see what the city council decides

123

to do."

He put on his hat, a new white, low-crown, wide-brimmed cowboy type with a crease down the middle. "All five of my men wear hats like this. Got them yesterday. I've got a man outside. He came on about eight this morning. When you leave, he'll be behind you, so don't shoot the guy. I don't want you to lose him. Just let him be a rear guard. No arguments."

He pulled her to him and kissed her hard on the mouth. She melted against him breast to breast, and the man knew that this kiss had been special. Ned Silver came away from her lips and stared at her a minute, grinned and kissed her again, lightly. Only then did he let her go.

"I don't want you kissing my man outside there that way, y'hear?"

"Not a chance, Ned Silver. Not a chance. I'll be back here around dark. Unless I change my plans. Might even get you some supper if you promise to be good."

"Can't promise, but I'll work at it." He waved and went out the back door. She saw him moving away from town along a little-used trail of a street; then he curved back the other way toward the downtown area.

What was she going to do this day? She would have to wear some kind of a disguise. She looked in the bedroom and found her suitcase sitting on the floor. She hadn't seen it last night. Everything that had been in her room at the hotel had been repacked inside. She found what she wanted: one of her loose-fitting dresses and a big hat with a floppy brim. She used a pillow and put it around her waist and tied it with a string. In the old dark dress and the big hat, none of the Mexicans would even guess who she was. The .44's wouldn't fit under the dress, so she compromised by taking her stiletto in her boot and the hideout .38 Colt Lightning double-action revolver.

She had sewn a pocket in the many folds of the skirt that held the little gun with the three-and-a-half-inch barrel.

The .38 slug didn't have the stopping power of the .44, but it could do a lot of damage close in. She looked in a mirror, and satisfied with her disguise, she slipped out the back door. Rebecca saw the man in the white hat sitting under the shade of a lonesome tree half a block away. She slowly meandered down the alley in back of the house, taking the same general route that Ned had. She knew her protection was back there, but she tried to forget him.

Her first stop was at the Prescott General store for a box of .38 ammunition. She had used up her last box in target practice and had only the five rounds in the weapon. She told the clerk that they were for her husband's gun and she hoped they were right. The clerk assured her they were.

She fumbled her way out of the store and left the clerk shaking his head.

Back on the sidewalk, Rebecca watched the people. She saw half a dozen Mexicans lounging around, going nowhere, watching the people closely. The nearest one didn't give her a second glance. She found her shadow three stores back evidently interested in the contents of a window showing tin ware.

She saw small groups of people, mostly men, talking about the no gun law and the saloon closing. The booze problem seemed to upset the men the most.

Rebecca watched for the Chicken, the skull-faced man who had shot down the woman and her daughters on the train. She had decided he would be the first target. He must move around town. She watched every Mexican she saw, but he didn't turn up. Perhaps he had been wounded seriously the other night when she shot at the second gun in that first attack.

At last she went to June's Cafe and sat down at the counter. She asked for June, and when she came,

Rebecca moved back the brim of the hat so that the woman could recognize her.

June nodded. "Come on back, you can't sit out front. I had six Mexes in here this morning watching and waiting. They had coffee and left."

Once they were safely inside the back office, June brought coffee for them, and they sat and talked. It was a slow time in the cafe. Rebecca's guard with the white hat came in for coffee.

"I'm hunting the Mexican man who is so thin his face looks like a skull. I've heard he's called the Chicken."

June laughed. "He's easy to spot, but he hasn't been around. I hear he got himself shot."

"Fatally, I hope," Rebecca said.

"Not that bad. I'll watch for him. If he's around town, I'll see him. He drinks at the Mex cantina, but you can't go in there, men only and Mex whores."

The cook called, and June scowled. "Duty beckons. You stay here and cool off and rest a bit. I've got some good apple pie I'll bring in. Right now I got to do some out-front working."

Rebecca waved at her and took a deep breath. It was good to sit a minute.

Ned Silver faced the five Taos city councilmen in the back of the Jackstraw Saloon. Each man had a cold beer at his side, but there was none at Ned's place at the table. He nodded at them as he came in the room and sat down. At once the lawyer, Owen Johnson, came to his feet.

"Mr. Silver. You were hired to come to town and do our bidding. That doesn't seem to be how it's going here. No one told you to dig out all of our old laws and start enforcing them. As the city council, we absolutely refuse to let you do that. There are some items we want to go over with you that you will implement at once."

"No!" Ned Silver's voice boomed into the closed room, and the lawyer looked at him in surprise. "Sit down and listen to me. You five hired me to come here and do a job. You don't know how the job needed to be done or you wouldn't have sent for me. The blind leading the blind. It can't be done that way.

"I've walked your town. The first thing you need to do is get the people involved in Taos. Most of them don't give a damn about this place one way or the other. You've got to get them involved in city government to make anything happen.

"That's what we're doing. When you take away a right a man thinks he has, he gets mad; then he gets involved, and then things begin to happen for the good.

"Don't tell me what I can and can't do. Read the contract. It states that I will enforce the laws of this town. I'm doing that. I'm closing up the saloons at eight P.M. the way the law of this town now on your books demands, and there will be no guns carried in public in the town after today at six P.M. and henceforth.

"My men and I and the county sheriff, who has a contract to provide law enforcement for the city, will enforce those laws even if a city councilman shows a firearm."

"You're fired," the lawyer said. "We want you out of town on the stage that leaves first thing in the morning."

Ned Silver laughed. "Mr. lawyer, read my contract. You can't fire me. I'm the law in this town for thirty days, and you know it. You wrote the damned contract.

"Now, to other matters. What did you decide about Mr. Montrose and his problem with the Indians?"

The council members stared at each other.

"Can he do this, Owen?" Josh Randall asked.

"I'm afraid so. The contract is specific."

"God damn!" Lynn Keating said. "So all we can do now is ride it out for thirty days and see what happens."

"What about Montrose?" Ned Silver asked again.

"We offered the Indians three beef a month for two years," Webb Bryce said. "Montrose was going to pay. Gray Squirrel refused flatly. Said it was a matter of principle now."

"So now it's between Montrose and the Indians."

"Why don't we call in the army from Santa Fe?" Lynn Keating asked.

Ned shook his head. "The army doesn't mix in civilian matters anymore. Congress passed the Posse Comitatus Law in 1878 that keeps federal troops from interfering or aiding local civilian authorities in any civil law matter."

"But this is Indians killing a white man," barber Olson said.

"They haven't yet," Ned said. "Might not. It would take an uprising by the Pueblo to get the army up here. They still have to police and fight the Indians."

The council members looked at their lawyer.

Johnson nodded. "He's right. Not many people know about that law yet, but the army sure does. They won't touch a case like this."

"Now, gentlemen, I would suggest that you support me on these law enforcements. They are the way to operate right now. If you want to hold open council meetings, invite the public in, and discuss the business of the city openly, I'm sure that you'll see in a hurry what the general population wants. At that time you can wipe out the old laws on the books or alter them. In the meantime, I'm enforcing them to the letter."

He stood and watched them. "Was there anything else you gentlemen wanted to talk to me about?"

The five sighed and shook their heads. Ned nodded at them, picked up his white hat and walked out into

128

the saloon.

"Public city council meetings?" Keating roared when the door closed.

"Yes, gentlemen, that's in our Taos city charter as well," Johnson said softly. "It's like the old New England town hall meetings. The people can talk on any topic they want to."

"We won't get anything done," Bryce wailed.

"What we do is establish an agenda of things to talk about and work on," the lawyer said. "That list is posted a week in advance, and those wishing to talk on those subjects register with our city clerk; and then they can talk. We can't bring up anything that isn't on the published agenda."

"Damn, getting complicated," Olson said.

"Looks like we've caught ourselves a tiger by the tail with this Ned Silver," Bryce said. "We do it his way for thirty days, then we'll see what happens."

Rebecca had been wasting time, stalling all day. At last she had worked out a plan. There was nothing she could do in daylight; but the darkness would cover her tracks, and she could then make her first assault on the colonel's fortress. At least she could do some scouting work and check his in-close security.

She had a sandwich with June at midday, then talked to Ned a minute to let him know she might be late getting back to the house that night. Then she spent an hour buying some soft, silky underthings at the only store in town that catered to women. She left them there, paid for them and said she would pick them up later. Her white-hat man sat in a chair across the street watching her.

Leaving the things at the store saved her going back to the house again.

At six that evening, she walked the streets, watching the sideshow. The six white-hatted regulators, including her guard, swept down Main Street, stopping every male they saw with a firearm. The first three shrugged, said they forgot and went quietly to jail. The next two tried to run. They were stopped.

Ahead of the regulators, Rebecca saw a growing group of men walking away quickly or heading for the alleys to get out of the way. The regulators continued their sweep of Main Street, herding along with them a group of peaceable men they had arrested. On the way back, they caught four more and came to the county jail with twenty-two men. They were quickly processed and put in the jail cells.

Ned Silver and his regulators went out for another sweep through the street, but this time found only one man with a firearm. He had staggered out of a saloon and into their arms. He was the first man taken to the ice house.

"Hey, Silver. I feel safer already," some wit called from a group near the general store. The regulators quickly checked the men and found half a dozen holsters but no six-guns.

Rebecca sat in front of the barbershop in a chair watching the show. As long as the men stayed inside private businesses, they were not subject to the gun law. Once they stepped to the street, they were.

Darkness slowly enveloped the streets of Taos. Rebecca nudged the Colt .38 nearer to the outside of her skirt where it would be easy to get to and turned down the block to walk to the small house that Ned Silver had rented. She found it easily, walked past it and down the alley, then doubled back and went in the unlocked rear door.

At once she lit a lamp, drew the Lightning DA and checked the small house. No one lurked there. In the bedroom she changed clothes quickly, putting on a black pair of pants and a dark brown shirt. She had combed her hair out that morning, but now bound it into tight rolls on each side of her head. She didn't want to take the time to braid them.

Once outside, she settled the twin Smith and Wesson American .44's in leather and walked quickly toward the Mexican section. She wasn't sure if her body guard was still with her or not. She hadn't seen him since the gun sweep on Main. She went a different direction and came at the big house from the far side.

She slid past the usual clutter of small-frame houses and tumbled-down shacks at the outskirts of the section, then came to better houses. When she was two blocks from the castlelike headquarters of Sinfuegos, she spotted a roving guard. He slouched against a house and smoked a cigarette.

She crouched in deep shadows and watched him. He scanned the street, then walked half a block down and came back. He was gone nearly five minutes. It would be simple to put him down, but she didn't want them to know she had been here. Not yet. First she had to find the key to getting into the Sinfuegos' fortress.

When the guard made his next trip down the block, she slipped past his post and moved through shadows and cover until she found the next guard. This one was not smoking. He carried a rifle over his shoulder on a strap and had a revolver at his hip.

He walked a beat as well, but it was no more than thirty feet each way from a scrub tree at the side of a well-tended house. She could see the outline of the big house half a block beyond.

Rebecca felt around on the ground beside the house where she crouched until she found two rocks about the size of crab apples. She spotted a tin roof on a shed three houses down. She waited until the sentry turned to walk away from her, and she stood and in one smooth motion threw one of the rocks high over the guard's head toward the tin roof.

It fell short. She walked into the street and threw the second rock as hard as she could. While it was still in the air she ran silently, Sioux fashion, across the rest of the street and at right angles to the path of the guard.

The rock hit the tin roof, and she saw the guard rush forward. Another man down that same street hurried up from the other way.

By that time she was well past them and working silently through the shadows of the larger houses. A light flashed in one of the houses, then moved as if someone carried a lighted lamp.

She wedged against the side of a house as two men walked down the street. There was no boardwalk here, only the dirt of the street and the house porches. They passed without seeing her, and she moved ahead.

Now she could see the big house. It had a fence around it, a white picket one for show. She watched the barrier and the side of the house for half an hour. In that time she saw two guards. They walked around the fortress spaced evenly. That left the spot immediately in front of her free of any guard for about twenty seconds.

She checked it again, counting slowly as the one man vanished around one side and before the second man came within sight of the area from the other side.

Twenty-two seconds. Where would she go? There were shrubs around the house. Behind one of them she saw an open window.

She timed the guards again, then imagined herself running to the fence, vaulting over it, rushing to the shrub and crouching behind it without a sound or motion as the guard walked past less than three feet away. Yes. It could be done.

She smiled. She had an entryway into the place. Could she get in, kill Sinfuegos with her knife and get out of the house without anyone seeing her? Did the man have a woman, or several women, he slept with? What about servants who lived in? Were there guards inside? She needed to know a lot more before she tried to assault the place.

She also needed some equipment. She would make some of her special roofing-nail grenades. Yes, they were defensive as well as offensive. Tomorrow she would get the dynamite, or have someone else get it for her. June could help there. Yes. And the roofing nails. She would bring the sawed-off shotgun. She could tie it on a cord around her neck.

As quietly as an aspen leaf floating down on a moonlit lake at midnight, Rebecca slipped back the way she had come. She couldn't use the rock this time on the closest guard. Instead she tried timing it. The fraction of a second that he turned to walk away from her, she sprinted down the darkened street, flashing past the intersection and into the shadows of the first house. He had just turned when she stopped, frozen in place.

The guard paused, and she could imagine the frown on his face. He had seen something out of the corner of his eye, but not enough to cause him to sound an alarm. A cat maybe, he could be thinking, or one of the mongrel dogs that roamed the night looking for scraps to eat.

She moved on down the street in the darkness, passed the next guard with no trouble and was soon jogging back toward her house.

She checked the North Star and found the Big Dipper. The two pointer stars on the Dipper bowl showed her that it was only a little after midnight. Good.

Ned should be in the little house by now waiting for her. She smiled softly into the night and hurried a little faster.

CHAPTER 13

The next morning, Rebecca wore her floppy hat and dark dress again. There was no bodyguard. They agreed it wasn't needed. She went to the store and bought roofing nails, the one-inch length with the big round head, then some strong sticky tape.

Her next stop was at June's Cafe, where she talked in the back room to the owner. June grinned.

"Damn right! I have a kid who does errands for me. He'll get the dynamite for you. How many sticks you want?"

"Twenty sticks should be enough, along with fifteen blasting caps and ten feet of burning fuse. That'll do it."

June's eyes shone. "Damn, I wish I could go with you. I've always dreamed of paying back some of these sons-of-bitches who take a girl for granted. That bastard Sinfuegos, right? Christ, I'd love to be there when you blast him into little bitty pieces!"

Rebecca grinned. "It might not be quite that satisfying, but it will be a first strike on his fortress."

They heard some yells and a few screams outside. Both hurried to the door and looked out. Five horsemen came abreast down the street. It took a few moments for Rebecca to realize that they were Indians. Pueblos! She hurried outside and watched as the five walked their mounts down Main and stopped in front of the Inter-Mountain Freight Lines office.

Rebecca saw three of the white-hatted regulators following the scene from the sidewalks. Ned was one of them. He watched as the Indians waited in front of the freight line office.

All five of the warriors carried rifles.

"Hey," someone in the crowd shouted. "They got rifles. Why don't you arrest them, Silver?"

"They're not citizens," Silver shouted back. "So I can't arrest them. I have no jurisdiction over them."

One of the Indians slid off his bareback mount and walked slowly toward the freight lines building. It had a large door that a wagon could back up to and unload.

A moment before the Indian got to the opening, a horseman charged from the door.

"It's Montrose making a run for it!" somebody in the crowd screeched. Montrose took the Indians by surprise and was fifty feet ahead of them before they got their mounts into motion. The Pueblos were not good horsemen, would rather trade a horse than keep one. Since they normally stayed in one spot, they had little use for horses except for occasional long trips to hunt for deer, elk and buffalo.

A moment later the five Indians rode out after Montrose. He headed out the Santa Fe road.

"Well, that's one problem the town is going to have solved soon," Rebecca said.

"Yeah, but what'll happen?" June asked.

"Five Pueblo Indians after one frightened white man who is riding his horse to death means it will be over soon. Knowing a little about the Pueblos, I'd say they have already had a council and condemned Montrose. Now it's just a matter of riding him down and killing him."

June looked up. "He's eaten here. I liked the man.

135

Doesn't it bother you that he's going to be killed?"

"No. He's a killer. The law should have taken care of it if the laws were up to date in New Mexico. But the outcome will be the same here. He killed an innocent, so he should die."

June frowned. "I hear that you've done some killing yourself, Rebecca."

"That's right, but never a man who didn't deserve it. I have no regrets."

"Oh, I didn't mean that—"

Rebecca touched her shoulder. "I know, I understand. I wonder how Montrose is doing."

Montrose saw the Indians coming. He had a horse saddled and waiting. In the saddlebags he had all the cash that he owned. He had withdrawn it from the bank yesterday. He left instructions with Owen Johnson to run the business until he got back.

He cursed himself that he hadn't left last night just after dark when he first planned. Now he'd have to run for it. He had two pistols and a rifle, all loaded.

He saw the Indians lined up out in front. When one slid off his horse and started toward the door, Montrose kicked the big mare in the flanks, and she burst out the door into the street.

"Hiiiiiiiiiii!" he shouted to the horse, and in a few seconds he was past the Indians and racing south for the Santa Fe road. Yes, he'd make it. His horse was rested and ready. He got the best running mare that the livery had. Paid forty dollars for her.

He knew the Indians had rifles, but most of them didn't know much about the weapons. They didn't like to use them, still preferred their bows and arrows.

He spurred the horse into a steady gallop and looked behind. The Indians were coming but at a gentle trot. Why weren't they rushing after him?

he wondered.

Then he realized it would be a long chase. If he kept his horse running this fast, she would break down in a mile or two. On foot he wouldn't have a chance.

He slowed his mount, turned a small curve in the roadway and for a moment was out of sight of the heathens. Should he slip off the road and ride down the creek a ways? That way not even an Indian could track him in the water.

But he would have to come out sooner or later, and they would follow the banks until they found that spot. No, he'd try to put some distance between them and maybe set up an ambush. Could he kill all five of them with his rifle before they overran him? Maybe. It was better than running all the time. How far would they chase him? They didn't seem to have any food. Then he realized the Pueblos could live off the land, crickets and grubs and rattlesnake meat.

He patted the mare's neck. She turned and looked at him a moment, then back at the road. It was a good wagon road, no problems there all the way to Santa Fe. Then he'd get a train out of there and arrange for Johnson to sell the business for him. He wasn't sure where he'd go.

Now all he had to do was outwit these stupid savages. Yeah. He'd put his time in on the trail and in the woods. He wasn't exactly a tenderfoot. Think, he had to think how he was going to do it.

First he settled the mare down to a ground-eating canter. Then he watched the landscape. He'd need cover; he'd need surprise. An ambush was the best bet. He'd find a spot where the trees and brush came close to the road so that he couldn't miss. Yes.

The mare's eyes flared, and she snorted, then stopped short and shied suddenly to the left as if she were cutting out a steer. Montrose hadn't been watching the road and wasn't ready for the sudden move-

137

ment. He hadn't ridden much lately either, and the sudden turn surprised him.

One foot came out of the stirrup, and before he knew it, he plunged out of the saddle to his right. He hit the dirt hard on his left leg and hip. His leg bent under him, and he could hear the bone crack as his weight slammed down on the twisted leg. He plunged forward and screamed in pain.

He was disoriented, and his head reeled from the shock and the sudden fall. When he opened his eyes, he screamed again. Not more than two feet in front of his face lay a rattlesnake coiled and ready to strike.

The snake must have been what spooked the mare, and now the rattler eyed Montrose as if evaluating the danger of this large creature. Montrose tried to remain still. When this near to a rattlesnake, the secret was not to move a muscle, and soon the snake would uncoil and slither away.

He couldn't do it. His arm was under him and hurt like fire. His left leg bellowed in pain at him, a burning, jagged edge of agony.

Montrose stared at the snake and then could hold his head up no longer. It dropped to the dust of the wagon road.

At once the snake struck, the fangs penetrating the softness of the man-thing's neck. In the fraction of a second the fangs sank into his flesh, the deadly venom gushed out.

The triangular head withdrew, and the coil formed perfectly again. Montrose screamed, and the snake struck again, this time hitting his cheek, gushing poison out.

Montrose wailed now and tried to sit up. The rattler struck him twice on one arm, then once more on his right leg as it came around to relieve the pain of his broken left leg.

The snake recoiled and watched him now, its darting forked tongue testing the air, waiting.

The rattler sensed the vibrations in the ground again; more of the big animals were coming. It knew the vibrations and usually tried to avoid them. This time there was a more important matter: the big animal in front of it. Was it dead or might it still present danger?

The mare had moved off the roadway and searched for blades of grass or high country graze.

The heavy vibrations came closer.

Montrose looked up as the five Indians rode up and circled him and the snake. They chattered in their native tongue for a few moments; then one of them dropped off his horse and picked up the revolver which had fallen from Montrose's holster in his spill off the horse.

The same Indian took his rifle and clubbed the rattlesnake, killing it with two sharp blows to its head. Then the Pueblo Indians got off their horses and sat on the ground, watching Montrose.

"Christ sakes, you going to shoot me or what?" Montrose screamd at them. He could feel the poison spreading through his system. His neck already felt hot, and he was sure it was swelling.

He saw his arm swelling around the snake bites. Christ, what had gone so wrong? He was just trying to keep his business going. That damn fake deed and the Indians and the burial grounds. Damn. Why him? Sure he had shot the Indian in a wild rage, but that wasn't enough to punish him this way!

"What do you want?" he screamed at the Indians.

Hawk Caller shook his head. "Mr. Montrose, we want nothing from you. The spirits of the sky and the sun have spoken. They have put their friend the rattlesnake in your way. Did it spook your horse and make you fall?"

"Yes, dammit, I need a doctor. That snake struck me five times before you got here. Help me!"

"No doctor could help you, Montrose. The poison

139

is traveling too quickly through your bloodstream."

"Then, at least give me some water to drink. I'm burning up."

Hawk Caller did not reply. He only stared at Montrose.

"You're just going to sit there and watch me die? That's worse than killing me, you savages!"

"You are the savage, Mr. Montrose," Hawk Caller said calmly. "You are the one who killed a Pueblo Indian in a fit of anger."

"Oh, damn!"

The sunshine faded for a moment, and Montrose knew he had to get back on his horse and ride into town. He struggled to stand. He forgot and put pressure on his left leg and screamed. He fell down twice before he got the knack of standing on one leg and hopping toward his horse.

He tried calling her but didn't know her name. She wandered another six feet away. He was thirty feet from her now. He hopped twice more. The extra pressure on his right leg was paining him. His left leg dragged behind him like a sea anchor.

Twice more he fell. Each time, he got up, sweating and swearing and watching the Indians who sat there watching him.

After nearly a half hour, he got within five feet of the mare. She snorted, eyed him a moment and ran off thirty yards, tossing her mane as she went.

Montrose fell onto the ruts at the side of the road and cried. Tears welled up, and he let them flow. The pain had lessened, but so had his ability to use his right leg. It had swollen now as well and felt so hot.

He tried to wipe the sweat off his face, but his left arm wouldn't work. He saw how it was swollen, and it was red and hot to his touch. The damn poison.

For a moment the sun faded to a dark gray, and then gradually it came back. He was losing his sight!

Twice more the sun blacked out entirely, and

Montrose wailed in fury and desperation.

"You who talks English. Help me for God's sake! Get me on a horse and rush me back to town."

There was only silence.

He had fallen facing away from the Indians, so he couldn't see them. He couldn't turn to look at them. Slowly his head sank, and he found he couldn't hold it out of the sand and dirt of the edge of the roadway. His neck felt ten times normal size, and his cheek burned and pounded from the poison.

"Help me!" he cried once more.

He looked up as he sensed movement. The Indians had come again. This time they stood in a small circle around him, dark eyes watching him, faces impassive. They were waiting for him to die.

"I'm not going to die you heathens!" Montrose bellowed. But the bellow came out as only a whisper. The sky lost its deep blue. He could barely see the legs of the Indians.

Slowly the whole scene was touched with a light gray; then it got darker and darker. Montrose screamed one more time, but no sound at all came from his paralyzed throat.

The poison worked faster now. His lungs labored to continue pumping air. His eyes closed. He could see nothing. He lay there aware that he was still alive because he still could feel the raw agony of the pain in his broken leg.

What had he done wrong? Why him? Then it didn't seem to matter so much. Everything grew fuzzy in his mind, and the pain eased. He tried to swallow. He couldn't. But now it didn't matter.

He coughed once, and then gasped for air, but that didn't matter now either. For just a moment he felt at peace. Then he saw himself running onto the burial grounds and screaming, lifting the big revolver and shooting once.

The Pueblo Indian looked at him in surprise and

141

then fear as he crumpled to the ground.

Montrose couldn't make the agonized look in the dying Indian's eyes go away. It burned into his brain, and then at last it vanished. A long gush of air came from his lungs, and Maxwell Montrose no longer existed.

One of the Indians said something. One of the band hurried and caught the big mare Montrose had been riding. They put Montrose over the saddle, head and feet down, his arms hanging toward the ground. They wrapped the dead rattler around the saddle horn, and all mounted and headed back to town.

A block from the first stores of Taos, they whacked the mare on the rump and sent her walking faster toward town and her stall in the livery.

The Indians rode around Taos and hurried back to the pueblo. It was finished. It was done. The matter was closed.

Five minutes after the Indians left the mare, she walked into the center of town. Somebody saw her and ran and took the reins and led her to the sheriff's office.

Ned Silver came out and sent for Dr. Madden. Ned pulled the body down and laid Montrose on the boardwalk. Then he took the rattler off the saddle horn and laid it on Montrose's chest.

"Damn, look at his neck!" somebody in the crowd said. "He's been rattler bit, for damn sure." More people crowded around. One woman screamed and ran when she saw the rattler on the dead man's chest.

Ten minutes later, Dr. Madden finished his preliminary examination and stood. "No doubt about it, the man died from the rattlesnake bites. No other wounds on his body that could cause his death. He has a broken leg, that's for sure, compound fracture with the bones extending through the flesh."

"Yeah, but how about them five Indians chasing him?" a voice asked.

Ned shook his head. "We may never know. It isn't like the Pueblo to torture a man. They wouldn't catch a snake, break Montrose's leg so he couldn't get away, then turn the snake loose on him. Not like them."

"So what happened?" the doctor asked.

"We'll find out from Hawk Caller. My guess is that his horse shied at a snake on the road and threw him. He broke his leg when he fell almost on top of the snake, and it struck trying to defend itself."

Dr. Madden closed his small bag. "That's good enough for me. I'm writing up the death certificate as accidental death due to broken leg and rattlesnake bites."

Rebecca walked away from the group. It could have happened that way. She'd talk to Hawk Caller herself. She went to June's Cafe, and the owner motioned her to the back. There in one paper sack she had the dynamite, and the caps and fuse were in another sack.

"Be careful with that stuff; it can blow people apart," June said.

Rebecca nodded grimly. "It better!"

She took the sacks and the nails and tape she had bought earlier and hurried out of the alley. She remembered the silky, frilly things she left at the women's store and stopped for them. Then she headed for the house.

This time she walked well in back of the small house before she turned toward it and came up the alley and in the rear door. No one followed her. She had stopped three times and checked.

Now she took off the dress and put on her pants and shirt and spread the dynamite on the kitchen table. She found the sharpest knife in the drawer and carefully cut six sticks of dynamite in half. Then she cut each of the half sticks in half again.

With the sticky tape, she formed the four short

pieces of each dynamite stick together into a square and taped them securely. Then she laid out the roofing nails and taped rows of the nails around the square of dynamite.

When she was through, she had about thirty of the roofing nails taped to the three-inch length of four chunks of dynamite. She called the little bomb her roof-nail grenade.

Rebecca worked for an hour making up the six small grenades. Then she taped the remaining sticks of dynamite together without cutting them. She made three bundles of two sticks each, then made the last eight sticks into one big bomb.

When she was done with that, she took a lead pencil, sharpened the point and used it to gently work an inch-deep hole into each of the small bombs. Into that hole would go the dynamite cap that would set off the bomb.

Then she cut the burning fuse. First she cut off a foot of it and counted in seconds as it burned itself up. It burned a little faster than the foot a minute it was supposed to. That was acceptable.

She pushed a two-foot-long piece of fuse into the hollow end of the dynamite cap and laid it aside. That would be for the big bomb. She did the same thing creating one-foot-long fuses for the two-stick bombs, and then pushed three-inch fuses into the dynamite caps for the six small bombs. The fuses on the small ones would burn in about fifteen seconds. She kept the fuses and caps separate from the dynamite. She would push the caps into the bombs just before she used them.

She was ready. Now she just had to wait for dark, and she would pay another visit to *el Zopilote!* This one she hoped would be the last visitor he ever had.

CHAPTER 14

Josh Randall, Lynn Keating and Farley Nash sat in the back room of the Jackstraw Saloon. They each had two bottles of chilled beer in front of them, and they stared at each other with glowering expressions. It was after eight o'clock, and the saloon was closed. Nash had spent the better part of today in jail because he wouldn't close the Jackstraw, which he owned, last night at eight.

"Something has got to be done before he breaks every businessman in town," Nash said. He took a pull at the bottle of beer. The bottle had a ceramic top with a rubber washer that was held in place with a pull wire that had a pressure snap arrangement.

"Most of the merchants are screaming," Randall said. "Hell, I'm hurting as much as any of them. They yell at me about those laws being enforced because I'm on the city council."

Lynn Keating leaned back and drew on the long cigar, then blew three perfect smoke rings that lifted toward the ceiling.

"Way I see it is that we're stuck for now," he paused, and when the other two looked at him he continued. "Unless we take some kind of drastic action. I'm damn well in favor of drastic action."

Randall squirmed on his chair. "Just what kind of

drastic action, Keating?"

"Hell, any kind you want. The object is to get rid of Ned Silver as the ramrod of our town."

Nash began to grin. "You're talking about getting rid of the man . . . permanently?"

"Damn right, do it the right way. Nobody would ever know. Nobody would ever find the body. The other enforcers would shrivel up and move on. We don't have an iron-clad contract with them."

Josh stood and moved around the table where the big poker games were usually played. "I don't know. That sort of thing could backfire on us."

"Not on us, Josh," Nash said softly. "We won't have anything to do with it. I'll talk to a man who will talk to another man, who will offer a third man some kind of a reward for doing some target practice. If he hits his mark, he'll earn a year's wages."

"I still don't know. Be hard to keep it quiet. Besides, Silver never leaves town, so we couldn't lure him out in the country someplace. It would have to be done here in town."

"So, that's no big problem," Keating said. The rancher grinned. "Hell, some drunk from one of the saloons got pissed when his favorite drinking hole closed up at eight P.M., and he went after the man doing the closing. Neat, simple, and we won't be anywhere involved."

"Offer one of these drifters three hundred dollars cash money and he'd shoot his own mother," Nash put in.

Keating looked at the saloon owner. "You can set up the three levels of orders?"

"Hell yes. I give each man twenty dollars to contact the next man. That's forty dollars. So it costs us each about a hundred and fifteen dollars. Hell, I lost that much in gambling money last night."

Josh Randall sat down but squirmed and stood again. "Hey, it sounds good, but I've never done anything like this before. Killing a man really sticks in my craw."

"Think about your three businesses going broke, Josh. That would put a stick of dynamite down that craw of yours. Hell, this is the way to do it, the only way. I say we get it done tomorrow for sure. I can contact the first man tomorrow morning and make sure he gets a second man I don't know about. Then that man picks out a shooter who can do the job and will be out of town before his .45's barrel is cooled down."

Josh Randall sighed. At last he nodded. "All right, count me in. I just hope this isn't something that we live to regret."

Josh and Keating opened purses and wallets and produced the needed hundred and fifteen dollars. Nash added his and rolled the bills and put the gold coins in a special pouch he took from one of the drawers in the table.

"Yeah, tomorrow for sure," Nash said. "You won't know anything more about it until after our town tamer gets tamed down a little himself."

Rebecca decided to wait until near midnight before she made her attack on the Buzzard. Let them get to sleep, and the guards tired and sloppy. Yes.

She was pleased when Ned came in about eight-thirty.

"Town is as quiet as a church choir with laryngitis. The saloons all closed down right on schedule, and we found only four drunks with guns. We'll keep them in jail over night and haul them out of town on a wagon come daylight."

She told him about her plans as she cooked him some supper: mashed potatoes, brown gravy and some roast beef she had brought home from the meat market and had been cooking on top of the stove for

147

two hours.

"Not a chance I'm letting you go over there tonight," Ned said. "*Zopilote* still has too many guns. Sure, you got past two sets of guards; what about the ones inside? You can bet he has at least two men up all night inside. Even the two of us over there couldn't do the job without getting ourselves killed."

He kissed her and stopped her protest.

"We wait and get him whittled down a little. I'm going to start rousting some of his men tomorrow. Pick up ten or fifteen, take their guns and run them out of town on a wagon. Most of them are not citizens. He's brought in twenty guns from across the border for some big operation. So I'm legal to run them out."

"They'll just come back to his compound up there."

"Some of them. Some of them will believe me and keep on going back to Mexico. I can convince them. We get him cut down to half the guns he has now, and then we'll talk."

He picked up one of the small grenades made of dynamite and roofing nails.

"You must have used these before; they look horrendous."

"I've heard about them. Figured they would help even up the score a little."

Ned laughed. "Just a little. One of these could knock down ten men."

"What I was hoping."

He took second helpings of the mashed potatoes and brown gravy and the roast. "Why didn't you tell me you could cook, too?"

"You didn't ask. What about the city council? Won't they do something to stop you enforcing these laws?"

"I figure they'll hold a public meeting and repeal some of the laws we're enforcing, especially the gun

148

law and the saloon closing. But that takes a week."

"Will they do anything else?"

"Not much they can do besides blow me out of my saddle."

"Somebody tried before?"

"In about half the places somebody gets mad and takes a shot at me. Usually a spur of the moment thing. We're always on the lookout for it. Don't know if it'll happen here or not."

"It better not. If somebody kills you, I'll be upset." She saw him look up quickly, and she giggled. "Just wanted your attention. You want to wash dishes or dry?"

A half hour later the kitchen was cleaned up, and they stood looking at each other.

"You ready for bed?" he asked.

"It's just a little after nine-thirty."

Ned chuckled. "I didn't say ready for sleep." He caught her arm then, picked up the kerosene lamp, and they walked quickly into the bedroom.

It was a little after nine A.M. when a ragged, dusty man struggled into town. He saw the saloons open and rushed inside the first one. At the bar, he ordered two cold beers and drank both down almost without stopping. He was dirty, and his clothes were torn; but he had put up cash for the beer. When he caught his breath, he looked around.

He spotted a man wearing a suit and slid into the chair across the table from the man. The gambler had just spread out a game of solitaire. He looked up, annoyed.

"Hey mister, you want to stake me to a gold claim? We can go partners, fifty-fifty. All I need is fifty dollars to get a mule and some gear and some food."

"Move on, old-timer, before I squash you like the filthy bug you are."

The old prospector shrugged and went to the bar-keep. He whispered to the man for several minutes; then the apron shrugged and led him behind the bar to a back-room office where the owner sat.

"Gold!" the prospector said. "Gold, more than I ever seen. A whole damn wall of it twenty feet high and lots more scattered on the floor of the cave."

The owner of the Homestead Saloon, Doug Cassidy, nodded. He heard a story like this about once a month, but he always listened; you could never tell.

"You brought some of it with you, this gold?"

"Well, no. Didn't want to cause a stampede, a gold rush, you know."

"So why should I believe you?"

"Remember we had some lightning storms a week ago. Really fired off up in the mountains. Well, one of them strikes hit Slash Mountain up there and caused a new landslide. The slide opened up an old entrance to an ancient cave. Older than the hills! Saw some wild stuff in there, but right near the front is this wall of gold!"

The saloon man finished his breakfast and put down a napkin. He knew about Slash Mountain, the common name for the sliced-apart gash on the side of one of the peaks. They did have a big electrical storm a week ago. Possible. He eyed the old prospector.

"You'll need a horse and a pack mule, some tools and food enough for two weeks. That's more than a hundred dollars' worth. I might stake you for seventy-five percent."

They settled on sixty-forty with the saloon owner getting the most. An hour later the story was all over town. Ned heard it in the barbershop as he had a haircut.

Rebecca had put on another oversized dress as a disguise and heard the story in June's Cafe. By the time the prospector had his horse and gear ready, there were twenty men with horses saddled and

150

canteens full waiting to follow him.

Ned had seen Rebecca at the cafe and talked to her.
"You heard the big story?"

"Did. This isn't prime gold country."

"True, but the old guy saw something. A cave back in there might produce gold. I'm going to trail along."

Rebecca laughed at him. "A fool's errand. How far away is the mountain?"

"Three hours almost due north, maybe a little more. Fifteen miles at the most."

She shrugged. "I'll see you when you get back."

He left, and so did Rebecca. She ran back to the house and changed clothes, putting on her pants and shirt and .44's. She added a low-crowned brown Stetson and then walked quickly an around-about way to the livery stable.

Rebecca saddled Šila and rode out. She went around the town and caught the tail end of a string of riders working north. She passed about half of them before she came to Ned Silver and one of his white-hat regulators.

"Figured I might as well give Šila a run; he's been cooped up in the livery too long."

Ned snorted but grinned as well. "Glad to have you along. Don't figure it's going to turn out to be much more than a ride, but can't hurt much."

Twice Rebecca saw brief glances of other horsemen moving the same direction. They were a half mile over and usually out of sight. She was sure they were Pueblos. They, too, must have heard about the gold find. Most Indians had no use for gold. Many called it woman's clay, because it could be used only to make pretty trinkets. It wasn't hard enough to make a spear point.

Why would the Pueblos be heading north when the talk was of gold? She said nothing to Ned about it.

When they came to a flat spot, she checked the trail. There were now more than fifty mounted men following the lone prospector at the head of the column. At least it would be a good outing for Šila. He was jittery and full of vinegar this morning, truly living up to his Oglala Sioux name meaning "the trickster."

They rode for three hours, and twice more Rebecca saw glimpses of the Indians. She pulled even with Ned and told him about the Pueblos.

"They must think there's something to it, or they're interested in seeing just where it is. We're well off the square mile of Pueblo land by now."

They rounded a narrow gorge that mothered a small stream coming down from the Sangre de Cristo Mountains and directly ahead saw the big slash on the mountain.

Some of the riders near them shouted in surprise. The slash was now twice as big as before, they said. Millions of tons of rock and dirt must have thundered down the face of the thousand-foot-tall slice of the mountain.

It took them an hour to detour around the pile of rubble that extended a quarter of a mile from the face of the slash. The old prospector worked around through the slopes and valleys and at last came to the place he wanted. He got off his horse and headed over a jumble of rock and dirt that was another fifty yards from the face of the cliff.

When Rebecca and Ned got to the cliff, they could see a ten-foot-tall hole that was apparently the opening of the cave. The prospector had just pounded in stakes and cried out in a loud voice: "No more place to stake a claim here, men. I'm sorry. I hereby claim this cave as a hard-rock deep mine by right of discovery." He grinned. "The rest of you might as well go home. Unless we got a lawman along, nobody else but me and my partner are

152

going inside."

Ned and Rebecca moved up to the front of the crowd, and Ned introduced himself.

"Well, good, Sheriff. You just come on in and verify this here claim with my partner. I brung me along some gunny sacks rolled up tight and wired on sticks. We can soak them in this here kerosene to make us some torches." He motioned Ned and Rebecca. "Come on now, I can't wait for you all day."

Ned and Rebecca moved up, and Ned took one of the torches. At the entrance to the cave, they had to walk down ten feet to the floor. The burning torches lit the way, and Rebecca was surprised how big the cavern was. She guessed it was thirty feet tall at that point, and she couldn't see the far side.

The prospector had stopped at the near side wall and held the light up. "Here she is, the bonanza I been looking for all my life. A goddamn wall of gold!"

Ned stepped forward and picked up a chip of the material that had fallen from the wall. There was a jumble of them around the base of the twenty-foot-high wall.

He studied it in the torch light a minute, then he shook his head.

"If this is what you came back for, you're in for a big disappointment. Have you ever seen real gold?"

The prospector pointed at the wall. "For damn sure, right there."

"Afraid not, my friend. That's iron pyrite. Most people call it fool's gold."

The old prospector's mouth gaped open. He ran to the wall and stared at it. Then he gouged it with a hunting knife. It was hard as iron.

Slowly he slumped down beside the wall and began to cry.

Ned turned away from him, held the torch high

and moved back deeper into the cave. He saw something along the wall and turned that way.

For a moment he and Rebecca stared at the six-foot-long shelf that had been cut into the solid rock. On it lay a scattered array of skulls and human bones. Around the bones were intricately made pieces of silver work and jugs and bowls of silver and turquoise.

"Is this what it looks like?" Rebecca asked. He caught her hand, and they moved carefully along the cave floor another ten feet to where the torch showed a second niche cut into the wall. On it as well were bones of some long-ago man, surrounded by silver and turquoise figures and finely made jewelry.

"Out," Rebecca said. "These must be Pueblo, and that line of warriors must be here by now. We better get out quickly and make our apologies to the shaman or Gray Squirrel, whoever is coming this way."

They took the still-weeping prospector and his partner saloon owner with them. Only a few minutes after they came out of the cave, a line of Pueblo horsemen picked its way almost to the top of the scrabble of rocks.

Gray Squirrel led them. He looked and saw Rebecca and signed quickly.

"Is this the cave of our ancestors?"

Rebecca said it was and that there was no gold mine here; the white men would all leave quietly.

"Get these white men out of here," Rebecca whispered to Ned.

He turned to the crowd of anxious miners.

"Sorry, men, it's been another wild chase after nothing. The bad light led our friend to think he'd found a wall of gold, but it's only iron pyrite—fool's gold. So it's time to turn around and get back to town before the saloons close."

The men growled and groaned, but when they saw

154

the old prospector in tears heading down the rock fall, they knew it had to be true and moved back to their horses.

Rebecca and Ned Silver stayed at the mouth of the cave.

"A burial cave," Rebecca signed to Gray Squirrel. "It might go back thousands of years. We leave you our torches."

They gave the torches to Gray Squirrel and two of his men, who went with him into the cave.

"Now, nothing for us to do but take a long ride back home," Rebecca said.

Ned nodded. "Yes, and there's a good chance that we'll get there before the saloons close at eight. One saloon owner was bragging today that he wouldn't be closing tonight at eight. I want to make sure that he does."

"Which saloon?"

"The big one, the Jackstraw, where the city council held its secret meetings."

They rode south.

CHAPTER 15

All but three of the fifty or so gold-rush riders had already arrived in town when Ned and Rebecca rode in. She had pulled the big hat down over her face as much as possible. It would soon be dark. By now she was sure the Mexicans knew that she rode the paloose horse with the spotted rump. She'd have to be careful.

She and Ned had just reined in outside the livery when a rifle snarled from less than fifty feet away. Dusk had settled, and it was hard to tell where the round came from. Ned slammed off his horse with a slug through his upper arm. He gritted his teeth to control the pain.

Ned had kicked out of the saddle and now hovered behind the big gelding, bent over and reaching for the rifle in the saddle boot. He was on the wrong side of the horse and couldn't get the rifle.

Rebecca had slid out of the saddle the moment the rifle sounded, dropped to the ground and sprinted for the hard side of a freight wagon parked just outside the big barn doors.

She got there without another shot coming and held both of her .44's at the ready. Another shot flared in the near darkness, and she pinpointed the shooter. She fired four times into the same area, then listened to see where the bushwhacker would be moving. He had to be going directly away from them. She saw just the mist of light-blue smoke through the increasing darkness.

She didn't have to figure it out; she just knew what to do. An old gunfighter had told her once that if a gunman had to stop and work out what to do next in a gunfight, he was already half dead.

She darted from the freight wagon to a light buggy twenty feet closer to the gunman. He didn't fire. She raced from there to a patch of brush another thirty feet ahead and roughly parallel with the position from where the man had fired. There was no reaction. She listened again.

Horses' hooves pounded as the last three gold-rush men came in from the ride. She strained her ears as she moved ahead into the light brush beside the livery. The brush led down to the small creek.

When the late arrivals had their horses inside the barn, she heard movement, then again. The gunner was heading directly for the creek. She went faster now, using all of her Oglala skills in silent and speedy movement through the woodsy place. Another thirty feet and she stopped, listening.

He turned downstream and was running. She ran too, making noise now, letting him know someone was after him. He stopped. She stopped. She was much closer. The bushwhacker ran again. She heard him cross the creek. She ran when he did.

There was no moon. The darkness was complete. She could hear the gunner panting. Good, he was not in condition. He would tire out and stop.

He ran again, down the slope away from town. She followed, careful to let him know she was still there to increase his panic. He cut out to the south road, and she followed. Now he ran like he was in a footrace along the open wagon trail.

Rebecca trotted along behind him, stopping at

157

intervals to check him by sound. She heard his panting; then the footsteps stopped.

She had run him to cover. But where was he?

Rebecca moved up slowly, silently as a winter breeze through leafless oaks. His gush of air came suddenly. He had been holding his breath. He was to the left, in the shallow ditch the rains had dug in the late fall.

He might have the rifle, and surely a six-gun. She squatted and studied the contour of the ditch. It was smooth and fairly even except for a lump about thirty feet down. It could be a rock—or a man. She found stones and began pelting the object with the hand-sized missiles.

The third one hit the object. It was the man, and he yelped. She followed the rock with a .44 slug, hot and sizzling. It bored through his right shoulder, and the man warbled in pain and anguish.

As soon as she fired, Rebecca darted six steps to her left. Quickly the bushwhacker fired where he had seen her gunflash. She shot again, and moved another six steps to the left. Her second round gouged through his left leg and brought another wail of pain.

"Give it up and live," Rebecca bawled in her lowest voice. She fired once over his head and moved. He said nothing for a minute, then screeched in pain.

"They'll kill me if you take me in."

"Probably, but even if they try, you'll have a chance at living. If you don't give up now, your chances of living through my next six rounds are absolutely zero."

"Goddamn!"

"You have until I count to ten." She started counting. When she got to five, he yelled.

"Stop! I don't want to die. My six-gun, I'll throw it toward you." She heard something hit in the roadway.

"Stand up and lock your fingers on top of your head."

"Can't, my leg is broken, I think."

"Stand on one foot. Do it now." She fired beside him, and the man rose out of the gloom and stood. He almost fell, then regained his balance. He was only twenty feet away now as she moved forward.

She came up behind him before he knew it. He nearly fell, but she steadied him. His hands remained on top of his head. She checked his holster, then looked for an ankle hideout and a boot knife. She threw away a four-inch stabber and patted him under the arms and down his legs. When she was sure he wasn't hiding any more weapons, she had him put his hands behind his back. She tied them there with a strip of boot lacing she had in her pocket.

"What's your name?"

"Lewton, Jay Lewton."

"Let's get back to town. I'm sure Ned Silver will have some questions for you. How much did you get for trying to kill Silver?"

"Three hundred."

"So you really were shooting at Ned Silver?"

"Yeah. Did I hit him?"

"Not sure, I'd guess you did. Who hired you?"

"Don't know his name."

She hit his shoulder with the barrel of her gun where her slug had bloodied his shirt. Lewton bellowed in agony. When he quieted, she asked him again with an even, deadly tone.

"Who hired you? I don't have to take you back to the sheriff alive, you know."

"Oh, damn. I never met the guy before. Barkeep said his name was Eldridge."

"Describe him."

"Short, maybe five-one, or five-two. Had a red beard close cropped and he's almost bald."

Rebecca pushed him on up the road toward the

lights of the livery.

"You just might have earned your right to go to trial for attempted murder. Should be worth at least fifteen years in the territorial prison."

Ned stood just outside the lights of the livery, waiting for them.

"Heard the shots. Knew I couldn't come down there or I might ruin it for you."

She saw the white bandage around his arm. "You got hit."

"Not too bad. What I want to know is who hired him and where I can find the bastard! I already put one of my men a half mile down the south road. He went around where we figured you were. I don't want anybody leaving town tonight until I ask a damn lot of questions."

They took Lewton into the jail and pushed him into a cell with blood coming from both his wounds.

Ned took Rebecca out to the front. "Look, lady. You've more than done your share tonight. What we've got now is straight police business. I want you to go back to the house and hole up until I come and get you. No more wandering around. I've heard that *el Zopilote* is getting crazy mad he hasn't caught you yet. Let's play it safe. I'll come by tomorrow."

At last she agreed. Ned woke up one of his white-hat regulators to take Rebecca home to be sure she got there safely. She frowned, but she knew she was tired. She waved at Ned and hurried out the door with the body guard.

Captain Quint Wonlander was on duty at the jail. Dr. Madden was not brought in until the bushwhacker told them exactly where Eldridge might be found. It only took five minutes as the man tried to control the bleeding.

Eldridge was probably at the bar in the Homestead Saloon. Ned went alone to find him. Eldridge had spent five of his twenty dollars of blood money buying beer for half the house. He could still stand up but was in no shape to answer questions. Ned took him back to the jail and Captain Wonlander looked at the drunk and shook his head.

"Ain't like Eldridge to have any money, drank himself out of his last job. The blood money cash fits the picture."

"So somebody hired Eldridge to find Lewton and pay him three hundred dollars to put a slug in me," Ned said. "Get him some coffee and some ice. We're going to get Mr. Eldridge here sober and talking if it takes all night."

It did.

He proved to be a tougher case than Lewton had. Eldridge came from the outlaw school of never informing on your friends, or the man who hired you.

About four A.M., Ned threw up his hands. "All right, Eldridge, all right. You don't know what we're talking about. We've got Lewton, who named you as having hired him to bushwhack me. I'm sure the jury will believe him, so you get fifteen years in the territorial prison."

Eldridge didn't rise to the argument. He sat in the jail cell propped against the wall on the bunk with no blanket. "Not a chance a jury will convict me. Lewton is a drunk, and nobody would believe him. You don't have a case that will stand up."

Ned laughed softly. "You're too sharp for me, Eldridge. So I guess we'll just have to settle it the old-fashioned way." He took out his .45 and checked the loads. Then he unlocked the door to the cell and swung it wide.

Eldridge didn't move an inch.

Ned went down to the end of the row of cells that had been emptied of drunks and gun holders, and opened the door to the alley.

"I guess it will have to be that you confessed, and then were killed while trying to escape. Happens all

161

the time. You'll even have a handgun, loaded, and be halfway out the alley door. Usually looks better if the door is unlocked and one of the jail people is wounded or hurt someway. That's me; you shot me in the arm." Ned Silver chuckled as he watched Eldridge.

"Right now is a good time. Four A.M. Nobody around. Only two of us on duty here in the jail. So, it's time, Eldridge. Now you're supposed to run like hell for the alley door."

"I'm not moving."

Ned shrugged. "Hell, don't make no difference to me. You tried to have me killed, which means you're open season for me. I can drag you down to the alley door just as easy if you're dead as if you're alive."

Eldridge wiped his hand over his nearly bald head and pulled at his red beard. "Look, maybe . . ." He shook his head. "Not a chance. He would roast my balls."

Ned cocked his .45 and leveled it through the bars, with the muzzle centered on Eldridge's chest. Ned drew back the single-action hammer, cocking it. His finger poised on the trigger.

"Makes no difference to me, Eldridge. You first, then that Lewton character. Two for the price of one. Damn, I hate a bushwhacker."

Eldridge scrubbed his face with his hand. "All right! Put the gun away. I'm remembering more about it. I think I can give you a name."

Ned didn't move. "Thinking you can and doing it are two different things, hombre. You either give me the name or you don't, and if you don't, my finger gets to stroke nice and easy on the trigger."

Eldridge looked at Ned; the icy green eyes stared back at him, unflinching, angry.

"Yeah, all right, I hired Lewton. He bungled the job. But that don't make me a killer. I got twenty dollars to find him."

"Who told you to do it? Who paid you?"

162

"Oh, damn. I'm moving on after this. A gent named Zed Younger. He's a clerk in a store somewhere here in town. I never knew him well. We did a stagecoach job once couple of years ago. Then he decided to give up the life and go straight and work for a living."

Ned turned to Quint Wonlander. "You know this guy Younger?"

"I do. He's a clerk in the tinware store. Does some tinsmith work as well. Told me once that he's getting ready to take over from old Ashworth once he learns the trade."

"Where does he live?"

"Don't know. Nowhere we can find out this time of night. First thing in the morning we can check with the postmaster in the general store."

Both men locked the prisoners in, stretched out on unused jail bunks and went to sleep.

Farley Nash sat in his saloon shortly after it was closed and long after he had heard about the misfire on the bushwhacking of Acting Sheriff Ned Silver.

How could it have gone so wrong? He had heard the gunplay and rushed down to the livery; but the man was gone and that damn White Squaw went after him.

It was more than an hour later that he heard that Sam Eldridge had been arrested just before closing time in the Homestead Saloon. He had made Younger tell him who the men were he had contacted. Nash wanted to know the string in case it got broken or something went wrong.

Something definitely had gone wrong. He didn't put much past the likes of Ned Silver. He'd do anything to a prisoner to make him talk. Which meant the law was just one step away from arresting Farley Nash. Never going to happen.

He took the derringer from his desk and checked to

be sure that there were two .45 rounds in it. Then he left the saloon and walked down the block and over one, then down another to the small house where Younger lived. Younger hadn't married yet. He was only twenty-four and had wanted to play the field and pick the goodies while he could, as he put it.

Nash went to the back door, knocked and waited for Younger to come. He might have a lady friend there tonight. He didn't, and the slender man with the pinched features grinned and waved Nash inside.

"What the hell happened?" Younger asked. "I did my job. Lewton didn't do his; I can tell by your expression."

"Not only didn't he do his job, he's been captured, and now Eldridge is in jail as well."

"Damn!" Younger said. "I'm getting out of town."

"You're getting away farther than that," Nash said. He pulled the small derringer and pushed it into Younger's chest and fired before the thin man could ram it aside. Younger grabbed at Nash as the bullet jolted into his chest. There wasn't a lot of power behind it, but the round tore through his lung and lodged in his back.

Nash frowned, moved the weapon and fired the second round into Younger's heart. Both shots left round powder-burn marks on Younger's white shirt. Couldn't be helped. Younger slumped to the floor this time. He lifted one hand; then it fell, and Zed Younger was dead.

Farley Nash nodded and stepped to the lamp on the living room table and blew it out. He picked his way through the room and then through the kitchen and out the back door. He looked around. Nash couldn't see anybody in the darkness. He walked down past the rear doors of three houses, then back to the street and to his house. He needed a good night's sleep. Things would look better in the morning.

CHAPTER 16

Rebecca had been in the small house for about an hour. It was just past eight-thirty, and she had made herself some sandwiches from the left-over roast beef and boiled some coffee.

When her supper was over, she cleaned up the kitchen and was about to go to the living room when she thought she heard a knock on the back door.

Rebecca drew one of the .44's from the holster over the back of a kitchen chair and slipped over to the back door. The knock came again. Standing beside the wall, she called out.

"Yes, who is it?"

"Juan" the soft reply came.

She frowned. Juan? Juan? Did she know anyone named Juan? Then she remembered the young boy on the road the two white toughs were roping. She edged the door open and saw Juan in the splash of light from the kerosene lamp.

"Juan, come in. How did you find me?"

"They know. *El Zopilote* knows where you are. He and some men are coming soon to hurt you. You must leave now."

She frowned. "Juan, this is important. You wouldn't lie to me, would you? *Es verdad?*"

He shook his head. "No lie, is true. They are

165

meeting now. Bring your things. We must hide you quick."

"Juan, why are you helping me?"

"Nice White Squaw help Juan. So Juan help her. Quick!"

She sensed his urgency. At once she knew he was telling the truth. Somehow they had tracked her here. She left two lamps burning in the house. She threw everything into her bag which still held her rifle and shotgun. At the last minute she pushed all of the bombs into her suitcase, and they ran out the dark back door.

She sent him home, saying she would be fine. They must not find him there. Juan left quietly, rushing away in the darkness.

There were only two houses nearby, one about fifty feet away, another one in the same direction twice that far. No other houses or buildings were on the block. None to the north of her. She found a spot about fifty yards north of the small house and put her suitcase there. Then quickly in the dark she assembled her rifle from the suitcase and laid out a dozen rounds for it.

She was still in her pants and shirt. She tied the sawed-off shotgun around her neck, loaded in two double-aught buck rounds and put another ten in her pockets. Then she laid out the six small bombs and gently inserted the detonators with their fifteen-second fuses into the holes she had made in the bombs that afternoon with the pencil.

She was ready. She didn't expect them to strike for a while yet. They might wait until midnight.

She lay there for two hours watching the house. Then she saw two dark figures slip up toward the front of the house and two more from the rear. They splashed something from tin cans on the door frame and porches, then threw burning papers on the fluid, and it blazed up quickly. Kerosine.

She watched. A dozen more shadows ran up now and formed a ring around the burning house. They were going to wait for her to come running out of the inferno and then cut her down with handgun rounds. The fire crept up the sideboards and caught on the roof. Some of the Mexican men moved around, impatient. She heard voices calling back and forth.

Five minutes later the entire four-room house was a cauldron of flames. No one had come out. A moment later the roof fell in, and the men stood up from where they had been lying down. Voices became more curious. Where was the woman?

With the rifle, Rebecca fired quickly and picked off three of the attackers before they knew what was going on. She was out of range of their handguns and remained in her position.

Six of them ran toward her, and she dropped two of them before they got in range of their revolvers. The remaining four retreated. She heard four more coming in from the side. There was no fire there to silhouette the attackers. She waited. When she figured they were within twenty yards, she lit one of the fifteen-second fuses and held the bomb for five seconds, then threw it directly at the slowly advancing Mexicans.

She heard a sharp exchange of words; then the bomb went off, and the men screamed in pain and terror. Only one of the attackers limped away toward the rear.

She picked up two more of the bombs and cocked the shotgun and walked in a gentle arc in the darkness to the left and around the still-bright flames of the small house.

Six of the Mexicans had approached the flames, but now faded back out of the light of the fire.

She thought it strange that no fire alarm had sounded, that no curious had come. Then she considered the amount of shooting and the explosion, and she decided everyone was afraid to come out.

She waited thirty yards to the side from where she had been and slid in behind some small wild bushes. Four men crept through the sparse vegetation toward her. She figured they were angling toward her former base position. They would come within thirty feet of her.

Rebecca waited until they were directly across from her and lifted up and fired both barrels of the shotgun. She dropped down and reloaded, then rolled a dozen feet to her left.

The four men who had been trying to flank her position writhed on the ground. Three of them died outright; the other one could only crawl away with the .32-caliber-size balls deep in his arms and legs.

She lay there for an hour, and no one else approached either position. By then the fire had left a jumble of blackened stud walls and still fiercely burning floor joists.

Rebecca picked up her spare shotgun shells and walked back to her suitcase. There would be no one lying in wait for her. Her Oglala Sioux senses had not seen or heard anyone approaching this direction.

The last thing she had seen were ten or fifteen of the dark shapes moving back the other way away from the fire. She didn't believe that they had taken their dead with them.

At her suitcase, Rebecca broke down the rifle and put it back in the bag, then checked her loads in the shotgun. She left it hanging by the cord around her neck and put all but one of the dynamite bombs in her suitcase.

There was only one place she could go where she would be safe. Not the hotel. She carried the heavy suitcase in stages, moving away from town, circling around and coming up to the pueblo just below the plaza. She found one ladder still down offering access to one of the houses.

It took all of her strength to climb the ladder to the first floor of the houses lugging along the suitcase. She put it against a convenient wall and pushed the last bomb inside, then climbed two more ladders to the fourth level. There she stretched out on a mat outside a wall, held her shotgun and tried to go to sleep.

Here she felt safe. Not even *el Zopilote* would violate the privacy of the pueblo and come here looking for her. His men had suffered enough for one night. They would be back in their houses licking their wounds, binding them up and counting their dead and wounded.

The bastards! They had intended to roast her alive and then cut her to pieces when she jumped out a window and ran for her life. They had been paid in kind.

She turned, rested her head on her hand, lay on her side with her knees pulled up Oglala fashion, and she slept.

Ned Silver came awake promptly at six-thirty A.M. as he always did and got up from the hard bunk in the first cell. He tucked his shirt in his pants, washed his face but didn't bother shaving as he headed for June's Cafe. He'd seen a sign that said it opened at six-thirty.

It did. He had breakfast and was waiting at the general store when the owner came to open up about seven A.M. He said that of course he could tell the sheriff where Zed Younger lived.

"He's in the second house on Third Street, just a block down from the blacksmith. It's a white house with a small cherry tree in the front yard. He's renting it."

Ned adjusted his gunbelt, thanked the merchant, and marched down the street. He didn't trust the

169

boardwalks this morning; they made too much noise. He wanted to come on Younger as a surprise and to take him with no gunplay. This one he wanted alive so that he could be hanged later.

Ned turned at the blacksmith's and saw the house ahead. Only one house had a tree in the yard. He went toward the front door, then changed his mind and slipped around to the side of the house to the back door. He saw no one through the windows as he went past. No smoke came from the chimney. Good, Younger had slept in.

Ned tried the back door. It was unlocked. Ned eased it open and stepped into the kitchen. Nothing moved in the house. There had been no breakfast preparations. He could see a slice of the living room through a door. It was the only other exit from the kitchen.

Ned moved softly across the faded linoleum floor. He had out his .45 and held it with the hammer cocked. He flattened against the wall and slowly edged around so that he could see through the open door.

Nothing showed along the near wall. He moved farther and could see the whole living room.

A body lay on the floor beside a dining room table. The man was on his back with one hand on his chest. Ned didn't see any blood. Alive or dead?

Ned took three quick steps toward the man, but he didn't move. Ned bent and lifted the man's arm. It came up slowly, and when he released it, the arm fell gradually back to the chest. On the man's white shirt, Ned saw the two perfect circles of powder burns, one over his left lung, one over his heart.

Whoever this was, he was as dead as an alley cat under a freight wagon's iron wheel. The body was stiffening, rigor mortis. That meant he had been dead for ten or twelve hours.

Quickly Ned searched the rest of the house. No one

170

was there. He left the house and jogged back to the jail, where he woke up Quint Wonlander. Three deputies were already there, and the prisoners were yelling for some breakfast.

"Quint, you know Zed Younger?"

"Seen him enough. Yeah, I know him."

"Come take a look. I'm afraid somebody has just cut down the next man in our chain to find out who tried to bushwhack me."

They took Dr. Madden with them, and Wonlander confirmed that the man was in fact Zed Younger.

Quint Wonlander scratched his head. "Looks like that stops us from finding out who hired Younger."

"Maybe, but not for certain," Ned Silver said. "I'm going to have another little talk with our friend, Sam Eldridge. Younger might have said something that could tip us off. We might even give Eldridge some special privileges if he can point us toward the man who did hire Younger here in town.

Quint nodded. "If he can, we'll nail us another killer."

Dr. Madden looked bleary eyed. "Hope to hell this is the end of it. You know about the burned-out house and the dead Mexicans?"

"Burned house, where?" Ned asked, suddenly wary.

"Out to the north. Three Mexicans came to me last night with bad gunshots. Big fight out there about something. Mean to tell me you gents didn't hear it?"

"We were busy at the time," Ned said. "Point me in the right direction; I'll go take a look."

Five minutes later, Ned ran up to the burned-out house where he had sent Rebecca only hours before. As he came up to it, he saw two bodies sprawled in the dirt. Another lay twenty feet ahead, and he saw another one in front of the house. All were Mexicans.

He ran to the smoldering remains of the house.

171

Nobody could have lived through a fire like that. Did she get out in time?

He saw a procession of Mexican women pushing carts, coming toward the spot. He stopped them.

"The dead must remain where they are until I finish my investigation," he said.

A bright young man maybe fourteen translated what the lawman said, and the women sat down to wait.

He found another body on the other side of the house. That was five. They looked as if they had been shot with a rifle. Could have been Rebecca defending herself. The Mexicans could have attacked the house, torched it, and she killed five before she got away.

If she got away!

He circled the place looking for a spot where a rifle might have been used from the outside.

It had to be to the front. There he found some trampled-down grass and six spent rifle casings. He stood and searched. To the right of that position were three more bodies. He looked at those and snorted. Two of the men had roofing nails driven into their faces and foreheads. The third dead man had twenty of the nails slashed through his body, taking off the side of his face, ripping out his throat.

Ned Silver let out a long sigh of relief. Rebecca had not died in the house. These three dead were from the dynamite and roofing-nail bombs she had made. These dead men were the result of the deadly vengeance of Rebecca Caldwell. She was alive!

He looked on the other side of the house, then circled back and found the three dead men there. They had been splattered with double-aught buck. He knew the telltale signs.

Eleven dead. Even *el Zopilote* would be stunned by such a loss. All that from one little bundle of woman not as big as a minute!

He shook his head and walked back to the Mexican women. He motioned to the youth, and he came forward.

"What's your name?"

"Juan."

"Do you know what happened here last night?"

"Much gunfire, an explosion, more gunfire. Many dead."

"Who lived in the house?"

"I am not from this part of town."

Ned nodded. "Tell your people they can claim their dead. Will you bring me a list of the names of those killed? I'll need it for the records."

"*Si*, I can do that. I have the writing. To the *policia* station?"

Ned nodded. He was so damn glad that Rebecca was still alive that he really couldn't feel sorry for the dead men. They had come for a live *gringa* roast and shooting party. Instead, eleven of them had died. Now all he had to do was find Rebecca. He would put it down as a fight among two factions of the Mexicans. God knew they deserved their fate. Nobody in town would argue with his decision, especially the Mexicans.

He walked slowly back toward the jail. Rebecca. Where would she go? She said June at the cafe had become a friend of hers. But she would not know where June lived. If Rebecca had been hiding in the cafe this morning, surely she would have talked to him.

Where else?

Late at night, hotel out of bounds, she knew no one else in town; what would have been her first choice? The pueblo. He turned and walked quickly in that direction. Ned Silver was still fifty yards from the plaza in front of the pueblo buildings when someone hurried down the last ladder to the ground and ran to meet him.

Rebecca!

"Thank God you're safe," he said, catching her in his arms and hugging her tightly.

"More credit goes to a young Mexican boy named Juan," she said. She told Ned about meeting the young boy and how he came and warned her.

"I met him this morning. He came with the women to pick up their dead. Eleven."

They stared at each other for a minute. "I'm calling it a feud between two Mexican factions in town."

"*El Zopilote* will be furious."

"Good." He watched her. "You better stay here for a while. Not even the Buzzard will look for you here."

She nodded. "Come up and talk with Gray Squirrel a minute. He's astounded by the burial cave the old prospector found. He says the remains of his ancestors in the cave could date back a thousand years."

They climbed to the fifth level of the pueblo and went down through the roof to the house. Gray Squirrel had cold water for them and bean cakes. He greeted them warmly, then through signing told them about the cave.

"We have found priceless relics of our past. Finely made silver bowls that are decorated with turquoise. On some of the walls are pictures the ancients must have drawn with charcoal and bird-egg coloring perhaps.

"We have counted twenty-eight burial shelves, which could be for as many as twenty-eight generations, or even longer. We have no way of knowing how long the cavern was sealed by the great rock slide of Slash Mountain. Perhaps a hundred years, maybe five hundred. My people have always talked about Slash Mountain for as far back as our picture scrolls go."

"Are you guarding the cavern?" Rebecca asked.

174

Gray Squirrel told them he had four warriors with rifles guarding the cavern day and night. They were living inside the cave. In the far reaches of the cavern they had found a small spring of pure water that they were using.

Soon Rebecca explained her predicament to the chief.

"Gray Squirrel, there are bad men who tried to kill me last night, burned down the house where I stayed. I escaped."

Gray Squirrel smiled. He signed quickly. "As you escaped, you killed eleven of the Mexicans."

She nodded. "Can I stay with my brothers here in the pueblo until my work here is done?"

"We will be honored to have *Ŝinaskawin* stay with her cousins the Pueblos for as long as she wishes."

CHAPTER 17

Rebecca asked Ned to stay until she was settled in her new "house" in the pueblo. Gray Squirrel said there was a three-room unit on the second level that was not occupied. They looked at it and found the three rooms on the same level; one had a doorway built into it instead of a rooftop ladder.

The doorway was simply an opening in the form of a squat "T" with the vacant space smaller at the bottom, then stepped out on each side. The top was low enough a person had to stoop over to get in. At the top of the opening was a "curtain pole" where a blanket could be hung to shut out the weather.

The house had pegs and poles on some of the walls extending from the roof which could be used for hanging up clothes and blankets or baskets of food.

Rebecca explained to Ned that the blankets were rolled out on the floor for sleeping at night and shaken out and hung up during the day. The Pueblo people spent most of the day outside, with the rooms mainly for use at night or when the weather was bad.

One of the rooms would usually be used for storing food and firewood and other items the family would need for the long winter.

Since the growing and harvesting season wasn't over yet, most of the men of the pueblo were in the fields near the small stream where they irrigated their crops of corn, beans, squash, and pumpkins. It was the women's work to dry meats, fruits and berries.

Ned looked around at the Spartan accommodations and yearned for a chair or a good bed. At least they were alone. He bent and kissed Rebecca's cheek, and she turned.

"We're alone here; no one will bother us," she said. She took one of the blankets from a peg on the wall and draped it over the pole on the small doorway, then arranged on the floor two more of the blankets that had been woven by members of the clan.

Rebecca smiled and sat down on the blankets and began to unbutton the fasteners on her shirt.

"Ned, I've been missing you so. Last night I wasn't sure that I'd ever see you again. Now, come here and make all my preparations worthwhile."

He grinned and sat beside her, his hands catching her firm breasts and caressing them through her shirt. He helped with the buttons and pulled off her chemise, then bent and kissed her breasts until the nipples surged full of hot blood and stood tall.

She moaned softly. "I think we should get my new house here off to a good start. Are you so busy you can't take off an hour or so to tend to the needs of one of your temporary citizens of Taos and the pueblo?"

Her hands rubbed along his crotch, then upward to his fly, where she found the serious swelling. Deftly she undid the buttons there and worked through his underwear until she claimed the prize.

Ned had to clear his throat before he could speak, then he laughed softly.

"I think the county can spare me for an hour. This is a damned hard floor here, no feather bed."

"Remember, my introduction to making love was on an Oglala brave's floor. He said I wasn't worthy of his bed, so it was the floor until I proved myself. I think I can prove myself to you."

177

He pulled one of her breasts into his mouth and chewed slowly as she worked his turgid maleness out of his pants. She bent and kissed the arrowed, purple head, then eased it into her mouth and pumped back and forth a dozen times.

He caught her shoulders and slid her down on her back, taking her talented lips off him before he lost control.

Quickly then they took off the rest of their clothes. There was no window in the room, and in the soft half light they lay side by side on the blankets over the hard floor.

He kissed her breasts again and she shivered. Her breath came faster now, and she gripped his erect manhood and pushed his hand down between her legs.

"Touch me down there," she whispered to him. "Rub me."

His hand worked between their bodies, came up to her secret place and found the hard node. He stroked her clit one way, then the other, setting up a rhythm that soon had her grinding her hips against his hand. Her whole body trembled, and she held his mouth on her breast.

"Yes! Oh, darling, yes!"

At the same time she pumped hard on his lance, hearing him growing more and more excited.

"Faster, darling. Faster. Harder, stroke me harder. Yes, that's the way!"

As he speeded up, she did too on his turgid member, and a long low moan came from her, building and building until it was a cry of wanting and longing.

Then her whole body shook. She trembled, and then great spasms of relief and desire all wrapped in a sigh flooded her senses; and she jolted and shouted as spasm after spasm tore through her body. She pounded her hips against his, and then the climax trailed off only to be followed by another one just as potent and as long.

She pumped on his maleness faster and faster until he too cried out in total joy and fulfillment, and his hips bucked against hers six, then eight times, until he was drained and spent. Together they lay there totally exhausted, ready to die, panting like great steam engines to get in enough breath to satisfy their oxygen-starved bodies.

They lay together, neither wanting to move. At last he lifted her chin from his chest and kissed her.

"Amazing, fantastic, marvelous." He kissed her lips gently then came away. "Being with you is a constant series of surprises, do you know that little lady?"

She smiled, her cobalt-blue eyes teasing him. "Sometimes I surprise even myself."

"That's good." He closed his eyes. "Would you be angry if I caught a small nap. I was up until almot four this morning."

"First, don't you think that we've reduced the Buzzard's forces by now?"

"Yes, I think so." He closed his eyes, then snapped them open. "But not enough for you or us to make a full-scale attack on him." Ned smiled and his eyes fell shut, and he was sleeping in seconds.

She eased away from him and put on some of the lacy, silky underthings she had bought at the store, then donned her white elk-skin dress with the fancy beadwork. She put on the white, low moccasins and walked around the room, trying to decide just how to attack the Buzzard in his roost, and still get out alive.

The small bombs with the nails would help. With them she could clear a courtyard or a big room. But what about the lucky shot from someone she couldn't see? It was always hard trying to root a man out of a house, especially a big house with many rooms such as the one *el Zopilote* lived in.

179

She thought of the boy, Juan, but at once rejected the idea. Juan had saved her life. He had risked his own skin by coming to warn her last night. If the Buzzard knew of his trip, Juan would be shot at once as an example to the others.

No, she could not use Juan again.

June? She wondered if the cafe owner ever prepared any food and took it to the bandit's fortress. Probably not. What it came down to was her own abilities, her own knowledge and understanding of the white-eye's and the Mexican's minds, and how outlaws of both groups worked.

Wait. What had Ned Silver said? Something about arresting and booting out of town Mexicans who were not American citizens. He said *el Zopilote* had brought in a group of gunmen from Mexico for some big project.

If she could catch him and some of his men out in the wilds of New Mexico, even in the mountains, she could deal with them on more even terms.

But what was his big project, and when would it take place? Juan. Juan might be able to find out without endangering himself. Might be able to. But how did she get in touch with Juan?

She heard shouts in the plaza, and she opened the blanket and looked out. She could not see, so she moved down to the next level quickly on the stone steps between the houses.

A horseman had ridden into the plaza. He was a Pueblo. Blood trailed down his shoulder to his waist and down his right leg. He nearly fell off the horse. Two women rushed forward and helped him to the ground. The shaman came out quickly and began binding up his wounds.

There was much shouting, and soon Gray Squirrel worked his way down from his fifth level and talked with the man. Rebecca hurried to the plaza as well, and when Gray Squirrel had finished speaking with

180

the warrior, he turned. When he saw her he began to sign.

"This is Much Corn. He was one of our guards at the sacred burial cave. Last night they were attacked by Mexicans, and the other three were killed. Much Corn pretended to be dead as well since he could not overpower them. Six men came with torches and used sacks and carried away most of the silver and turquoise bowls of our ancestors."

"Where did the Mexicans go?"

"Much Corn followed them, well back. They did not go to the usual Mexican section, but to a small house on the other side of town from the *bandido*. Two of them stayed there, and four went on to their homes in the Mexican section."

Rebecca screeched in anger. "Aiiiiiiiiiiii! What will you do?"

"We must take ten warriors and go to this white-eye lodge and fight the Mexicans and take back the relics of our ancestors. We must go at once!"

"I will come with you, and the sheriff as well. He is resting." She hurried up the ladder and then the steps from one level to the next and found Ned Silver almost dressed.

"What the hell's going on?"

She told him as he strapped on his guns. She picked up the shotgun, put ten shells in her pocket, and strapped on her six-guns over the white elk-hide dress, and they hurried down to the plaza.

"No time to get our horses," she said. "Can you ride bareback?"

"Learned to ride that way as a kid."

Within five minutes, Gray Squirrel came with ten warriors on horses, and mounts for his two friends. Each of the warriors had a rifle or a pistol. Most of the long guns were one shot; two were muzzle loaders.

Much Corn sat his horse, but there was pain etched on his face. Warriors rode beside him so that they

181

could support him on the horse if needed.

They rode north of town and came in from the east. Much Corn pointed out the house. It was partly fallen in on one side and looked like a place that someone had abandoned. Smoke came from the chimney. Two horses were tied in back.

Gray Squirrel was the war leader, and now he motioned for the riders to get off their horses. He sent four warriors up on the blind side of the house. Two more went on the other two sides. That left two warriors, himself, and the two white-eyes for the assault on the front.

They moved up slowly, using what little concealment there was. They were within thirty yards of the front door when they heard someone inside shout in Spanish. A small window in the door smashed outward, and a rifle snarled. One of the warriors snorted as the round missed him.

They had the shotgun and pistols. The shotgun could do some damage at that range. Rebecca fired one round at the door and window and heard the rest of the glass shatter and the door bulge inward a moment.

Gray Squirrel held up his hand. One of the warriors had scaled the side of the building and now stuffed an armload of long green grass and weeds into the chimney. He ran for a second armload others had thrown on the roof, and soon he stepped back and waited.

A shout came from inside the run-down house.

One Mexican man ran out the front door, wiping at his eyes with one hand and firing blindly as fast as he could with the other hand. Rebecca aimed and fired the second barrel of the scatter gun. Only two or three of the rounds hit him in non-lethal areas. He turned and ran directly at the two men at the near side of the house.

They knocked him down with pistol and rifle fire,

and he rolled over and didn't move.

It took longer to get the next man out. The men and Rebecca in front of the place ran forward until they were thirty feet from the front door. They began firing, sending a barrage of hot lead into the small house.

Rebecca used two more shotgun rounds, and now the spread pattern of the sawed-off weapon was small enough to be effective. Gray Squirrel held up his hand, and all firing stopped. They waited.

Five minutes later there had been no sign of movement from the house. Ned Silver leaped up and raced to the wall beside the front door. He made it without drawing any fire. The door sagged on one hinge. The bottom one had been shot away.

He put a sixth round in his .45, then jolted around the corner and into the house. A few seconds later he came out and waved them forward.

The other Mexican man in the room was dead. Evidently he had taken an early round through the head.

By the time Ned came outside and told Rebecca about it, a fringe of curious townspeople had assembled.

Ned told them the excitement was all over; they should go on about their business. They stared at the dead man, and one woman covered her face and hurried away. Three small boys walked up to the body and looked down at him a minute.

"Told you so!" one of them said.

"You didn't say dead as a doornail, so I win," one protested.

"Shot dead just like I figured," the third boy said before Ned walked toward them and they ran off hooting.

The Indians filed into the smoke-filled, tumbled-down house and carried out six gunny sacks filled with silver. The warriors mounted, took the sacks and silently rode away.

"What they carrying?" a man called.

"Indian property," Rebecca shouted back.

Gray Squirrel came out and leaped on board his horse like he was a young buck. He smiled and quickly signed to Rebecca.

"The Pueblo thank you for saving the bowls of their ancient ones. The cave still must be protected. It must be made sacred ground by the white-eye chiefs in Santa Fe. I hope that the Oglala White Squaw war woman will help the Pueblo and talk to the white-eye chiefs."

"I'll try, Gray Squirrel. The cave must be protected. Perhaps a small pueblo could be built there for the men who will have to guard it."

Gray Squirrel thought about it a moment, nodded and rode away.

Ned and Rebecca mounted, and they soon caught up with the warriors and headed back for the pueblo. Ned dropped off the horse near town and said he had to do some law work but he would be out to talk to Rebecca soon.

"I plan on having dinner every day at June's Cafe," Rebecca said. "I'll watch for you there. I'll probably be in the back room."

There was no more trouble as they skirted the north side of Taos proper and came into the plaza. The horses were taken away to the corral and pasture, and the artifacts were carefully stored in one of the rooms.

Rebecca went to her area and took off the elk-hide dress and folded it carefully. Then she put on the brown full dress and hid her .38 in the pocket and put her knife in her boot. The boots were covered entirely by the skirt which touched the ground. The floppy brown hat completed her disguise.

She hurried down the ladder and across the plaza. She still had to find out what the big operation was

184

that the Buzzard had his sights on. If she could find out when it was to happen, she'd have a great chance to attack him en route.

She came to the restaurant with no notice and slipped in the back door and waved at June.

"Hear there was big doings this morning," June said.

"Big enough for one day."

"Your house got burned up and everything."

"Yes."

June stood across from her. "I'd ask you to stay at my place, but I don't want to get burned up inside. How did you know they were coming?"

"Friends," Rebecca said and smiled.

They both grinned.

Rebecca had just finished the sandwich and cup of coffee for her lunch when a tall man came through the rear door of the restaurant. Rebecca couldn't see him well in the dim light. Then when he came close enough she gasped.

He had skin so tight across his face that he looked like a skull. He was the Chicken from the train. In his hand he carried a revolver aimed at her heart. The hammer was cocked, and he glared at Rebecca.

"Now, White Squaw, my turn to pay you back," he said in perfect English. "Out the back door, quickly, and don't try to get the knife in your boot. Señor Sinfuegos told me all about how good you are with it. It is now going to be my honor and pleasure to kill you so slowly that you will scream for the mercy of a quick death."

CHAPTER 18

Rebecca looked from the Chicken's skull-like face toward the front of the cafe, but June was not to be seen.

"She's busy with a flock of customers," the skull face said. "Get up slow and easy; keep your hands where I can see them. Then cross your arms in front of you and walk slowly out the back door."

Rebecca tensed. She could go for the gun in the pocket of the dress; but she was sitting in a chair, and he would see her.

"I can kill you right here if you want that. But where there's life, there is some hope. Move."

"You shot down my friend Aaron in that rail car. For that I'm going to kill you. Then you shot the woman and her two little girls for target practice like a crazy monster."

"Same way I'm going to shoot you, only a piece at a time. First I'll shoot your nipples off, close up."

They went to the back door. She still had the hide-out .38. She would find a chance to shoot him right through her skirt. She would make the chance happen. She would stay alive until then.

Outside he caught her arm and pushed the .45 into her side under his own arm so that no one could see it, and they walked along the boardwalk like lovers.

"I can scream for help."

"The second you do, my finger pulls the trigger, and you're dead."

"You wouldn't get away; somebody on the street would gun you down."

"It wouldn't matter to you, though, because, White Squaw, you would be stone cold dead."

"You're not Mexican at all, are you?"

"Never said I was. You guessed wrong."

He turned her at the corner, less than a third of a block down Main, and they walked out of the business area and quickly to the row of houses.

"Where are we going?"

"For a little ride. I want to see you naked in the cactus patches. You ever roll around naked in cactus before?"

"You plan on raping me before or after you kill me?"

"I don't need your hot little crotch, Rebecca Caldwell. I've got three Mexican girls who do anything I ask them to. They get downright inventive."

They went another block, then came to two horses. He boosted her on one and tied her wrists to the saddle horn. Then he mounted the other horse and led her animal as they rode north into the stunted pines on the hills.

It took them over an hour to get where he wanted to go. It was well above the Pueblo village, but in the same general canyon that fathered the foot-wide stream and the growth of brush and trees and taller pines.

He tied the horses, then unwrapped her wrists and let her down. He bent and caught her foot and dumped her on the ground. He searched her left boot, then her right, and found the knife. He nodded at the heft of it, then threw it into the brush. He didn't look for anything in her skirts. They tumbled around her crotch, leaving her bronze legs naked, but he ignored

187

her nudity.

"Get up."

She stood and kept her right hand near the hidden .38 Colt double-action revolver in her skirt pocket.

"Strip down to your waist. Come on, I want to see your tits."

He had the revolver out again, and by the way he handled it, she knew he was a practiced gunman. She undid the front of her dress, thankful that it held on to her hips despite the pull of the heavy revolver. She took off the chemise and held it. Her breasts glowed the light brown of her natural skin color with pink areolas and darker pink nipples.

The Chicken grinned. "Yeah, not bad. But two of my girls got bigger *tetas*. You think I can shoot your nipples off without nicking any of the white?"

Her hand edged lower toward the revolver. She forgot what position it was in. Would she be able to catch hold, get her finger in the trigger housing, and aim it at him all in one movement?

"Hell, let's try for the right nipple first," the Chicken said. "Stand sideways and throw out them beauties. I'll go for the right so don't flinch; it could be fatal."

She didn't think he'd actually try it. She stood sideways, and her hand moved slowly down to her pocket. It was hidden from him now since her right side was away from him. She worked her hand inside and caught the revolver by the handle. It was upside down. She had to turn it over, but before she could do that, the Chicken's six-gun fired.

She felt the wind created by the slug as it sliced past her breast. It missed her nipple.

"Damn," the man said. "Over corrected. Hell, I can't be worried about catching too much tit when I shoot. Push them out again. I'll do better this time."

He sighted in, and by then she had the hide-out turned so that she could aim it. Her finger was on the

188

trigger. Now, if there was only enough room for the double action to let the hammer pull backward and then fall. . . .

She had to turn a little more to get a good aim at him. It was like shooting from the thigh, not even from the hip.

He fired, and she felt a burning searing sensation. She looked down and saw a tiny drop of blood appear on the end of her right nipple where the hot lead had barely seared it on the way by.

"You bastard!" She turned a little more and pulled the trigger. The round from her Colt sliced through two folds of her skirt and smashed the back of the Chicken's right hand which held the .45. The weapon slammed out of his fingers, and he brayed in pain as the hot lead smashed and tore up a dozen small bones on the back of his hand before it exited out his palm.

He saw the smoking hole in her skirt, swore and looked at his gun six feet away. The Chicken turned and ran. By the time she pulled the Colt from her pocket, he was out of range. She started after him, slowed to pick up his .45 and hurried on.

A small smile creased her face. Now he was on her territory. No matter how good an outdoorsman he was, with her Oglala heritage and training, she was twice as good as he was. She pulled on her chemise, and then lifted the top of her dress and squirmed back into it as she followed the killer.

She saw him slide down a ravine, and by the time she got to the lip of it, he was out of sight. Which way? She stopped and listened. Only a soft sighing of the mountain wind came to her. She waited. She buttoned the front of her dress and arranged it, then listened again.

It was three or four minutes before she heard him move. He was heading downstream. Back toward the horses. She ran to them and sat down in the shade. He

189

came out of the canyon ten minutes later looking behind him.

She waited until he was within thirty feet of her, then using his own .45, she shot him in the right thigh. He screamed and fell, then struggled up and turned back toward the ravine. She ran after him, keeping him in sight at all times now, rushing when he ran, slowing when he walked.

Every time he tried to get back to the horses, she cut him off. She didn't waste rounds. She had two more in the .45 and four more in the .38. It would have to be enough. She could play cat and mouse with him only so long, then she would kill him.

He came out of the ravine and headed over a ridge and then turned up the canyon. He was limping badly now on his right leg.

She was aware he could get an avalanche started in the canyon, or simply throw rocks at her from overhead. She trotted to one side then climbed upward until she was at the same height as he was, but to his left. He lost sight of her for a moment, and when he saw her, he shrilled in pain and anger.

"Why don't you go ahead and kill me?" he screamed.

She didn't answer. It was harder for him that way.

His hand was bothering him now. He retied the kerchief around his right hand to stop the bleeding. Then he took another cloth and pushed it over the wound on his leg. Pain daggered across his face. He picked up a rock and threw it at her with his left hand. It went only halfway to her.

"What's the big raid the Buzzard has planned?" she asked.

His head snapped around quickly; then he shook his head. "Raid, hell, he's just trying to stay alive. He gave up on the train until he gets more men. You're causing him more trouble than he ever imagined."

They were twenty feet apart on the hillside. "How

190

in hell did you cut down eleven men last night all by yourself?"

"Because I wasn't trying to sneak up on somebody and roast them alive, that's how."

"A bullet doesn't care who fires it. That little bomb. How the hell did you make that? The hard part is getting them to explode when you want them to."

He stopped climbing upward and sat down. The skull-like face turned toward her.

"All right, I'm ready to give up. Tie my hands behind me and take me to jail. I'll answer to charges for the death of your friend Aaron and that Irish lass and her two daughters."

"I don't believe you. Once a rattlesnake with no morals whatsoever, always a rattler."

"A man can change."

"Not when he's still killing mad. Not when he wants to take my head in a bucket to *el Zopilote*."

The Chicken laughed. "You heard about that. Nobody could find you. What a bunch of dumb shits work for the colonel. When I got to feeling better, I found you in less than twenty-four hours. Too bad it wasn't a day earlier."

"You tracked me to the house?"

"Yes."

"Were you there last night?"

"Just far enough back so your rifle slugs missed me. I still don't believe it. I'm getting me a sawed-off shotgun. I like what they do."

"You don't deserve to live, you know that?"

"Told you I was ready to go to jail."

"That's a sham and a lie."

"Try me."

"Start walking back toward the horses."

He stood and limped down the hill. She wasn't sure how much of the limp was put-on. She hurried to keep up with him but stayed well away. She held

191

his .45 now for more range.

They got to the gentler slope, and she could see the horses two hundred yards away. She knew he was lying, but why? What did he hope to gain? She kept ten feet from him as they moved toward the horses.

"Yeah, I'll even walk back to town. You ride one horse and lead the other one. I'll be in front with my hands tied behind my back. That way I can't threaten anyone."

It was how she would have set it up. Where was the flaw in it, the trick?

"So come tie my hands," he said, the skull-like face staring at her from over his shoulder. She had the .45 trained on him as she moved closer. They were about one hundred yards from the horses.

"Reach out as far as you can with your arms to the side."

He did.

She walked closer. "I've still got your .45 trained on your back. One bad move and you're dead."

"Dead is one thing I don't plan on being. Go ahead, tie my hands."

She used her left hand to bring his left arm down and behind him. Then she looked at his other hand. She would have to reach across her body to get his right hand. She made the move swiftly.

In the few seconds it took her to reach across him to get his right hand, he whirled, grabbed at his pants pocket with his left and came up with a tiny derringer. He fired once from point-blank range, and the bullet seared her left arm.

His .45 bucked in her hand, and the round went through his side, cutting an inch of flesh, and ripped free. He spun and rolled and fired again with the derringer from ten feet away. The .38 round hit her thigh and dug into flesh.

The force of the round caught her off balance and knocked her down. She rolled and sat up, but already the Chicken was up and running for the horses.

She stumbled to her feet and tried to run after him. The bullet in her thigh hurt like fire. One round was left in the .45. She had to get close and make it count. He gained distance on her as they rushed across the hundred yards to the horses. She thought of shooting the nearest horse so that it would bolt and run away, but then she would have only the .38.

Rebecca gritted her teeth and swore softly under her breath as she ran. Each step on her right foot brought a new gush of pain from her leg. He gained more distance. Now he was fifty feet ahead of her.

She worked out the time/distance problem in her head. It would take him six or seven seconds to mount the horse and get it moving once he got there. She could run fifty feet in half that time.

Her leg hurt more. She slowed. He was almost at the horses. Sixty feet away! She beat down the pain, thought of his getting away free and lifted her feet higher as she ran. He gripped the horn with his right hand and screamed.

That slowed him getting in the saddle, and she stopped twenty feet from him and lifted the .45. The Chicken looked over at her a second before she fired.

His skull face seemed resigned, as if he knew he had lost. Then the round fired, and the skull-faced man slammed out of the saddle. His left foot caught in the stirrup, and the horse bolted, racing down the slope for town.

The outlaw had taken the bullet in the side. He wasn't dead as he toppled from the leather. Now he frantically tried to stop the horse as it galloped downhill, his shoulders and head bouncing and scraping along the ground.

She watched in horror yet fascinated as his attempts to stop the horse slowed and then ceased. His final scream came just before his head smashed hard against a large rock. Gradually the horse lost its original panic and began to slow.

Rebecca mounted the second horse and rode a hundred yards down the slope to where the other animal stood. The mare's nostrils still flared at the smell of death. Her eyes were rolling and wild. Rebecca came up to her on the side away from the body and smoothed her neck, patted her shoulder, and only then looked under her head at what was left of the Chicken.

His shirt had been torn off his shoulders and was gone. His head and face were only a battered bloody ball. Half the backside of his head had been ripped and grated away by the rocks and sand. None of his facial features could be made out.

She moved under the mount's neck and twisted the Chicken's boot out of the stirrup. Rebecca stared at the man for a minute, seeing again the woman's anger and terror as the Chicken shot her on the train. She nodded. One debt paid.

She took the mount's reins, stepped into the saddle of the other horse and headed back to town. Half of her mission here was accomplished. Now for the tougher part, *el Zopilote.*

She went back to town and left the horses at the livery, telling the yard man they probably belonged to Sinfuegos. Then she limped up the alley route to the back door of the jail. She still wore her brown dress, now badly soiled, and the floppy hat.

Rebecca gave the Chicken's six-gun to Ned Silver and told him what had happened. He called the doctor in, who said she would have to come to his office so that he could get the bullet out.

"I've got that new-fangled stuff, ether, and it works so fine you won't even feel me probing around in there."

"I've never had any of that ether," Rebecca said. "Does it smell bad?"

"Not for long."

194

"If Silver is there, I guess I can do it."

Twenty minutes later, the derringer .38 caliber bullet was pulled free of Rebecca's right leg, and she was coming out of the ether.

She stared at them for a second through foggy eyes, then turned her head and threw up. Dr. Madden had a bucket ready for her.

"Don't worry about it, almost always happens. Lots easier than trying to stand the pain of a bullet-ectomy." He laughed. "A little doctor joke there."

He bandaged her leg, told her to stay off of it for two days and then watched her hobble out the back door with Ned Silver.

Silver helped her mount the horse he had led her down to the doctor's office on, then grinned at her. "You mentioned that he shot you somewhere else. You didn't tell Doc about that."

She was feeling better. Her leg still ached with pain, but it would heal. She touched her right breast and scowled at the lawman.

"That other hurt is one that only your lips and tongue can heal, and you'll have your chance just as soon as I'm feeling a lot better. For now I'd be pleased if you let me use this animal so I can ride out to the pueblo and get a little bit of rest."

He watched her. "You evened the score with the Chicken, isn't that enough? You don't have to worry about *el Zopilote;* that's a county law problem."

She swayed in the saddle. "Whatever you say, *mi Capitan,*" Rebecca said. The way she grinned, Ned Silver knew damned well that she didn't mean it.

CHAPTER 19

Ned Silver let Rebecca go, convinced that she was too worn out and too tired to do anything foolish—at least for a few hours. He went back to the sheriff's office and helped Quint Wonlander finish writing up the paper work on the eleven Mexican deaths last night and then the two more this morning, and one for the man known only as the Chicken.

Two hours later, Ned Silver pulled up a chair outside of Sam Eldridge's cell and eyed the man. "Eldridge, you're looking at twenty to thirty years in the territorial prison unless you can remember something that Younger said when he hired you. Any hint, any stray name or word or indication, is all we need. There has to be a man who hired Younger, and that's the same man who killed him.

"That killer will be looking for you next just to make sure we can't trace the payoff back to him. Now think, man. You could be saving yourself a noose, a bullet in the back or at the least ten years in prison."

That got Eldridge's attention. He sat up on his bunk and began to reconstruct his hiring.

"I was in a saloon, let's see, yeah, the Jackstraw, the big one. Younger came up to me and gave me a cold beer and said we needed to talk.

"I'd seen Younger around a bit, knew him, kind of. The way he said it, I figured he had a robbery job in mind, maybe the stagecoach. I'm not against making an extra dollar here and there."

"What was the first thing Younger said after you sat down? Where were you, at a card table?"

"Yeah, in back, in the back room. He said nobody could overhear us back there. Well, I figured it was something big, something I could make a couple hundred for at least."

Eldridge stood and walked around his cell.

"Nothing of the kind. He just wanted me to pick out the best shot I knew who wouldn't mind making three hundred for a fast gun job. Just like that, he offers me twenty to find somebody who will make three hundred.

"I got mad, told him to find a gun himself. He jumped the price to thirty dollars and said the boss would be damned glad if I did this for them."

Ned stood up and stared at Eldridge. "You said that Younger told you that 'the boss' would be damned glad if you did this for them. You have any idea who this 'boss' might be?"

"Didn't know Younger that well. Don't know who he'd been hanging around with."

"Where did you see him?"

"Dunno . . . oh, yeah, at the saloon. Yeah always at a saloon."

"Which one?"

"Know that one for sure, at the Jackstraw. Let's see where else? Two or three times at the Jackstraw. Yep, seems like that's the only place lately I've seen Younger."

"Can just anybody go into the back room where you were?"

"Oh, damn no. That's for high rollers only. They don't get much business back there, but when it's busy, the money is big, damn big."

"So a regular customer couldn't just walk in the back room?"

"Not by a snotful, no sir."

197

"But Younger did. You said he took you back there so nobody else could hear what you talked about."

"Yeah, right. Yeah! But I didn't see him ask anybody if he could go back there."

"He must have already asked, or he was familiar enough with the setup and the owner so he could go back there whenever it wasn't being used."

"Yeah, maybe."

"Who owns the Jackstraw Saloon, Eldridge?"

"Not Younger, he's broke most of the time. Gent's name is . . . damn, let's see, I know it. Yeah, Nash, Farley Nash. That's the guy who owns the Jackstraw Saloon."

Ned left Eldridge stewing in the cell and talked to Quint Wonlander.

"Hell, not much to know. Nash bought the saloon three years ago, about the time I came to town. Been working with the city. He did object to the saloon closing law. We both were there when the boys tossed him into jail for the night. But, he's been closing up on time since then."

"He have any other arrests, any wild temper or emotional outburts? Anything like that?"

'Not on our books. First time he was ever in our jail was the first night of the saloon closing law."

"I'm going to pay the man a visit. Want to come along? I might need a witness." At the jail door, Ned motioned for one of the white-hatted regulators to follow them. He kept twenty yards behind the lawmen.

They found Nash behind the bar, spelling his apron for a few minutes.

"Well, Nash, I hear you've been closing on time, right at eight o'clock," Ned said.

"Yeah, and you know what I think of that law. Hell, it won't be on the books long. But for now, I can stand a short vacation from the long hours."

"I hear you got so mad about it you almost busted up your own bar."

"Wild rumors, Sheriff. I yelled a little, but I come from a long line of yellers. Ask my wife. Ask my barkeep. I've fired this apron I have now at least fifty times."

"An emotional man, I'd say."

"Some would."

"Where were you last night, Nash, from eight to nine o'clock?" Captain Wonlander asked.

"Where? I was here closing up. Lot of things to do after I get the last drunk out of the place."

"So somebody was working with you here until nine?" Ned asked.

"No, no the apron was the last one. He left about . . . oh, eight-fifteen or so, I'd say."

"I think I should tell you that we have Jay Lewton and Sam Eldridge in jail," Ned Silver said.

"So they won't be buying beer from me for a while. Why else should I care?"

"I figured you might," Ned said. "Also wanted you to know that I had a talk with Zed Younger yesterday a little after six o'clock. He seemed nervous and jittery."

Nash tried to light a cigar, but he couldn't keep the match steady on the end of the stogie. Ned reached over and held his hand firmly as he lit the big black smoke.

"So?"

"Younger works for you, doesn't he? Does odd jobs, throws out drunks when they get in the way. Handyman kind of."

"Not steady. Now and then."

"I asked him about the talk he had with Eldridge earlier in the day in your saloon."

Nash looked up. "But I heard you didn't bring in Eldridge until nearly seven-thirty that night."

"What difference would that make, Nash?"

"Wasn't that about the time you arrested Eldridge? What I heard. Small town, things get around fast."

"That's about the time," Quint said. "You mentioned that Younger knew Eldridge."

"I don't know if Younger knew this Eldridge or not. He probably knew a lot of people."

"Oh, he did all right," Ned said softly. "Fact is I talked to Younger that night about his deal with Eldridge. They said you were the man who set up the ambush and promised them three hundred dollars of blood money."

Nash leaned back slowly from where he had been standing behind the bar. His hands came up quickly, and they held a sawed-off shotgun he had slipped from a shelf under the bar.

"I don't know what you two are trying to railroad me into, but it won't work. I won't sit still and be tied into a murder plot. No, sir. Now, nice and easy the two of you take out them hoglegs and lay them gently on the bar. Do it now!"

He waited while the two lawmen removed their six-guns and put them on the bar.

"Now, hands. Lace your fingers behind your heads. Right now before my finger gets nervous on this trigger."

Both men stared at the twin, round, black holes of death in the form of the sawed-off shotgun muzzles and followed his orders.

"Now, out through the back door here; we're gonna take a walk down the alley, just the three of us."

"Not a chance, Nash!" a voice boomed from near the saloon front door. The regulator, whom Ned told to follow him, had just edged around the front door, white hat and all. The big .44 in his hand was leveled at the saloon owner. Nash looked that way, surprised, then squinted to be sure who it was.

As soon as Nash looked at the door, both lawmen dove for the floor in front of the heavy oak and mahogany bar and out of sight of Nash.

Almost at once, the shotgun went off. Mixed up in the thundering roar of the scatter gun came a .44 shot.

The regulator at the door had been partly hidden behind the partition of inch-thick planks. Most of the double-aught buck slashed into the heavy planks and stopped. One nicked the deputy's gun arm.

Nash didn't have any cover. The big .44 slug bored a straight hole through his heart and exploded out his back, dumping the saloon owner behind the bar dead before he hit the floor. A second round fired from the double-barreled shotgun shattered the ceiling as Nash's fingers spasmed in his death throes.

"Close," Quint Wonlander said as he stood. "So Nash was behind it."

"At least him and maybe some others, but it's too late now to get him to talk," Ned said. He turned and thanked the deputy white hat with a nod and a pointed finger.

"What about the other two in jail?" Wonlander asked.

Ned pushed the white hat back on his head an inch and pursed his lips. "I'd say you have a good case against them. I'll leave a deposition if the trial comes after I'm gone. They should get at least two years each in prison."

Rebecca Caldwell woke up four hours after she stretched out on the blanket in her rooms at the pueblo. She was slept out. For a moment she was confused about the time of day. The inside of the pueblo room was softly shadowed from the blanket over the door pole.

It wasn't yet dark outside. Rebecca stood and checked her leg. It hurt, but she could walk on it. The bullet wound had not damaged any of the major muscles. She had made up her mind about her next move. As soon as it got dark, she would pay a call on *el Zopilote*. It was his turn, and she was determined that he should have the chance to pay back society a little for all of the damage he had done.

She opened her suitcase and took out a clean pair of brown pants and brown shirt and stepped out of the dirt-clad brown dress.

Then she removed two of the two-sticks dynamite bombs from the suitcase. Carefully she took the tape off them and cut the sticks into four pieces each, then rebound them together to make the compact one-stick grenades. Around each of these, she wrapped two dozen of the roofing nails as on the others. Then she used a pointed stick and worked a hole in the four new grenades for the dynamite caps.

She had started with six grenades, used one and now added four more so she had nine of them. Yes. She made four more of the three-inch fuses and pushed them in dynamite caps and put them with the other detonators ready to insert into the bombs.

Now she had one big bomb of eight sticks, one of two sticks and seven of the grenades. She checked her shotgun, pushed in two rounds of the big man-killer double-aught buck and laid out twelve more shells. She wouldn't take the rifle or her hide-out. She needed a new knife for her boot, but it was too late to get one now.

Rebecca walked out on the patio of the house, which served as the roof for the first level below. A woman knelt behind a box next door grinding corn on her metate. She smiled at Rebecca and said something, then hurried into her house and came back with cold water and a bowl of soup. The soup was in a hollowed out gourd and was like many that Rebecca had used so long ago with the Sioux.

She urged Rebecca to sit down and then gave her the bowl and a white-eye spoon. Rebecca gave the sign for thank you, and the woman nodded. She came back with two slabs of cornmeal cake and then went back to grinding corn in her metate. Rebecca tasted the soup. It was beef, from the steer that the clan had recently killed.

As she ate it, she found it to be more of a stew than

202

soup, with beans and whole kernels of corn, chunks of beef and some other roots she couldn't identify. The stew and the cornbread and the water satisfied her hunger, and she thanked the woman again and took the gourds back to her.

The woman looked curiously at her pants and shirt. It was unusual dress for a woman. Rebecca went inside her room and sat on a slab of sandstone that formed a bench on the far wall. Usually it would be used for storing food and sometimes wood for the fireplace built into the corner opposite the doorway.

A large pottery water bowl sat in another corner, and there were pegs coming out of the wall where a weaving loom had once hung. For a moment she felt totally at peace.

She was with the People. She was surrounded with her ancient heritage. She was Indian again.

The feeling lasted only long enough for her to remember *el Zopilote,* and the terrible things he had been doing to his own people, and what he had tried to do to the Indians' sacred artifacts. That made her think of the other four Mexicans who had killed the three Pueblo warriors at the sacred cave.

It would be impossible to identify them now, but perhaps tonight she could retaliate in some small way for those three warrior deaths.

Rebecca was sure that Ned Silver had figured she would be up to something. He probably would come to the pueblo tonight looking for her. She would be gone before he got here, just to make sure he didn't try to talk her out of her strike against *el Zopilote.* This was a blow that she had to deliver.

She would be careful, cautious, go as far into the compound as she could and still retreat to safety with the aid of her grenades.

Dusk was not far off. She went back inside and checked what she would take with her. She utilized a small shoulder bag. It was a heavy cloth sack with a shoulder strap that would hold the bombs and could

203

be carried slung over her back out of the way.

She fitted the dynamite bombs in, pushed the detonators and fuses in her pocket, and then strapped on her Smith and Wesson American .44's. The shotgun would again go on a cord around her neck.

She grinned. For a moment she felt like a walking fortress. She had more fire power than lots of army patrols.

When it was fully dark, she left her house, stepped down the ladder to the ground and walked along the trail by the stream. It would take her closer to the Mexican section and at the same time avoid the trail Ned might use.

She walked about a quarter of a mile and sat down in a brushy spot where she could see the stream. It was too early. She didn't want to hit the Buzzard's roost until most of the armed men would be at rest. Then she would move in silently. If she could find *el Zopilote,* she would execute him for his many crimes against the people and for the deaths of the three Taos Pueblo guards at the sacred cave.

Her sleep that afternoon had left her refreshed and ready for the task. She had worked out a general plan, moving in much like she had before, quietly, and alerting none of the guards on her way in. If the same window was open, she would use it.

She listened to the chattering of the water. It would be good to sleep here, to let the water sounds lull her to sleep. She came alert, turned and had one of the .44's out in a fast draw, her eyes staring hard into the darkness up the path toward the pueblo.

"Easy, White Squaw, easy. Just old Ned Silver checking up on you." He came out of the gloom and sat down beside her on the grass.

"You didn't think I was going to let you go charging into the Buzzard's chicken coop all by yourself, did you?"

204

CHAPTER 20

Rebecca Caldwell scowled as she looked at Ned. "Dammit, you weren't supposed to find me."

"Nice ladies don't swear."

"Right now, I'm not a nice lady. I'm an Oglala Sioux war woman out on a raid."

"Yeah." He bent and kissed her lips. She returned the kiss and unhooked the shotgun and laid it aside. Then she reached around him. For a minute she held him tightly, then she eased back.

"Easy yourself, Ned, that comes after."

"Why not before?" he asked. "We have plenty of time. You didn't plan on going in until after midnight."

She looked at him sharply. "How did you know that?"

Ned chuckled and kissed her cheek. "Because that's the way I would play it myself."

She grinned. "We're a lot alike, you and me. You're right again; we do have plenty of time." She reached over and unbuttoned his shirt and pushed her hands inside, fondling his man breasts and caressing his bare chest.

He reached down and kissed her and quickly pulled open the buttons on her shirt.

"You make me feel so hot and wanting you so fast!

It's glorious!" She put her hands down to his crotch and found him already starting to harden. Quickly she opened the buttons and pushed down his pants and then his underwear until she found his treasure.

"Oh, my yes!" she crooned. "Out here in the woods and with the water gurgling over there, it's the way two people should always make love!"

He stripped down her pants, and his hand brushed the silky softness of her underwear.

"This is new," he said. "Nice, soft and delicate. I hope you don't mind my taking it off."

"If you don't, I'll shoot you right here," she said. There was an edge to her voice brought on by her passion. Her breath came faster, her breasts seemed to be on fire and she could feel the dampness at her crotch already in anticipation.

He slid the silk down her legs; then his hand found her secret place, and she moaned in delight as he brushed her swollen, tender nether lips.

"Now!" Rebecca demanded. "I want you inside me right now before I explode."

He thrust once, then twice, and they were joined; and they drove against each other, each determined to have satisfaction first. She gained the peak quickest and trembled as spasm after spasm tore through her, and she pounded against him to intensify the delirious pleasure.

Quickly then he climaxed as well, and they clung together there in the grass and leaves on the stream bank trying to paste themselves back together after the charge into ecstasy.

She reached up and kissed his forehead. "You are delicious, do you know that? How come you aren't married with about ten kids by now?"

He shrugged in the streaks of moonlight that penetrated the small trees and sparse growth of pine trees. "Just too busy, I guess. Worried about business."

"Probably chasing every pretty girl that you saw,

caught them, loved them and left them. Right?"

"Now you're talking from your experience the way you treat men. I don't see you married either." He kissed her lips so softly she barely felt the pressure.

They dressed leisurely, trading kisses and loving looks; then abruptly the mood turned serious.

"Things could get dangerous in there," Ned said. "I checked, and the feeling around town is that *el Zopilote* still has about twenty gunmen. He was supposed to get in some more for some big job, but they never came."

"Some train. He was going to attack a train, but the Chicken said he had given up that idea."

"Still, twenty guns is a damned army. What are your plans?"

Briefly she went over them. He nodded.

"Remember I ain't no Oglala in these damn boots. You'll move quicker and quieter than I can," Ned said.

"So we might have to take out one guard going in. We won't be visiting with the Buzzard for long. In, blow him to bits, and get out and away."

"With the Buzzard dead, his organization will fold up like a crumpled paper sack, and his men will all drift away to new jobs?"

"That's the usual story."

"What time is it?"

Rebecca couldn't see the sky. They walked out of the brush and trees and found the Big Dipper. It was not yet ten o'clock. They went back to the dell and talked softly.

"You ever been to Denver?" he asked.

"Several times. A beautiful little town."

"It's growing up, getting bigger now. Over thirty thousand people call it home."

"That big? Where do they get enough wood to heat the houses in the winter?"

"Mostly coal now. Maybe after this little bit of

207

business here is wrapped up, I could show you Denver. I know the best places to eat. There's always a play or a musical or an opera on stage somewhere in town. Would you like that?"

"Let's talk about that after we deal with the Buzzard. Sometimes I think planning too far ahead is bad luck."

"The Oglalas believe in luck?"

"Luck is the plaything of the gods. Treat them right and you will find good luck. Ignore the gods and your luck will be bad."

"That's pure Oglala."

They talked more, and he asked her about her time with the tribe. She told him the bad parts and the good, mostly good because she had adapted to the tribal life so quickly.

Sometime later, she tapped his arm. "It's time to go."

They moved as silently as wind gusts along the rest of the trail, then down a street and to the Mexican settlement. There was now a new guard a block from the two she had found before. He was not doing a good job, and they both slipped past him as he walked away from them.

The second guard was more alert. He had a post that took him about forty yards on each side of the street they used. Both dark shadows huddled against the wall of a house next to the corner as they watched him make his circuit.

When he was halfway down his forty-yard walk facing away from them, they rushed across the dirt street and past two houses into the next block.

The houses were mostly wooden frame, with an adobe here and there. The whites were now using adobe for building as well as the Indians.

The last guard before they came to the white picket fence of the fortress was the toughest. They found two men doing the same job one had done before.

208

Four men here, and with at least four streets coming into the leader's house, that could mean as many as twelve to sixteen men on guard duty.

"That will mean fewer guards inside," Rebecca whispered. They considered the two-man guard force. One was always watching the place where they had to cross the open street.

"We'll have to take both of them out," Rebecca said.

"Maybe there's another way," Ned said. "They both look so young, little more than boys."

"But they're working for *el Zopilote*."

"I heard that when the Mexican kids in town get old enough, he presses them into service whether they want to do it or not," Ned said.

The guard came closer. He was facing their way; the other one was forty yards away going the other direction. They had to silence both of them. One would do no good.

When the guard was opposite them, Rebecca rushed out silently, came up behind him, grabbed him around the throat with her arm and rushed him into the shadows on the far side of the street.

Ned had moved behind her, and now he clapped his hand over the youth's mouth. Frantic eyes looked up, then the eyes softened.

Rebecca looked at him and took Ned's hand off his mouth and relaxed her arm.

"Juan?"

He swallowed twice and rubbed his throat and then grinned. "*Sí*, Señor Sinfuegos put me on guard duty. I could not say no."

"We understand, Juan. I'm here to rid the town of this Buzzard. Will you help me?"

He nodded.

"What about the other guard?"

"He is older; he is devoted to the leader."

Rebecca frowned. "Go bring him here. Tell him

209

you found something you don't understand. Can you do that? I promise I won't kill him."

"Good, there has been enough killing. Let me get up now and finish walking my post. We'll be back soon."

Ned watched Juan walk away. "I hope that wasn't a mistake."

"It wasn't. Juan saved my life once; he won't get me killed now."

Juan finished his post and talked with the other guard. They both came to the deep shadows beside the house on the far side of the street. Ned had curled up on the ground, his arms thrust out as if he were dead. As the two guards bent to look at Ned, Rebecca came out of the shadows and slammed the barrel of her six-gun down on the other guard's head. He sank to the ground without a sound.

Rebecca quickly put a gag around his mouth, then bound his hands and feet.

"Tie me up the same way," Juan said. "Then if someone comes, I won't be blamed."

They did and a few moments later crouched near the last cover next to the white picket fence.

The guards here were as before, and Rebecca and Ned timed them on two circuits. The same timing. At precisely the right moment, they darted across to the bushes by the house. The window was closed, but they hoped unlocked, behind the bush. Just as Ned reached the window, the guard came in sight, and he rushed forward, his gun out.

Rebecca had planned ahead and was six feet from the window between the guard and Ned, still in the edge of the shrubs. She jumped out, surprising the guard, and her skinning knife sliced between ribs and through his heart. She dragged the man's body into the shrubs and out of sight. By then Ned had the window raised and was inside.

She slipped in beside him, and they closed the

window. They were in a bedroom. It was not occupied. They each lifted their shotguns and edged the door open.

Outside was a long hall with six doors off it. They couldn't clear each room. "Where is *el Zopilote?*" Ned whispered. Just then, a woman came down the hall. When she was next to the bedroom they were in, Rebecca jumped into the hall and pulled the surprised woman inside. One hand was over her mouth. She was a Mexican, young and well endowed.

"Donde esta el Zopilote?" Rebecca whispered to the woman, not sure if her grammar was right.

The Mexican girl pointed up with a finger.

Rebecca held up one finger. The woman shook her head. She held up two fingers and got a nod.

"Third floor," Rebecca said. They tied and gagged the girl, and then Rebecca gave Ned one of the grenades. She first put the fuse and detonator in place and gave him three wooden sulphur matches. He stuffed the bomb in his big pocket and brought up the shotgun. Then they worked toward the stairs.

Ned was in the lead. They were about halfway up the steps when someone came down. He was worried about something, and by the time he looked up, he was staring at Ned's eight-inch fighting knife. It drove in just over the man's heart, broke a rib when Ned twisted it and came slicing out through the guard's aorta. Ned quickly caught his collapsing form and quietly laid the dead man on the stairs.

They hurried on up, and on the second-floor landing found no one. At the top of the stairs on the third floor stood two guards. Rebecca blew them both down the hall with one round of the shotgun. Then they waited. A door opened down the way, and a bald head came out.

Ned put a .45 slug within inches of the head, and it pulled back in. They went down the hallway kicking in doors. There were only four of them. The first two

211

rooms were empty. In the third a cowering bald-headed man lay on the bed shivering.

They bypassed him, and one stood on each side of the last door. Ned was about to kick in the door from the side when a pair of bullets whizzed through the panel.

After the shots, he kicked the door in. Rebecca pushed her shotgun around the molding and fired one round. As the smoke cleared, they both peered through the wide-open door. They found only a room with two six-guns mounted on a desk and strings to the triggers.

The strings extended out an open window. Rebecca ran to it. The moment she looked out, a six-gun fired, but the round missed, slicing through a curtain near her head. She was sure the man had been *el Zopilote*.

"He's on the roof going down," she called. She lit the fuse of a grenade, held it five seconds, then threw it where she had seen the *bandido* vanish over the edge of the second-story roof to the first story.

The grenade went off ten seconds later with a roaring blast.

"Back down the stairs," Rebecca called. They rushed into the hall and found four men facing them. Rebecca triggered off the last round in her shotgun. The four men didn't have a chance to fire. Three of them went down in agony, and the fourth leaned against the wall, unable to move as they rushed past.

They got down to the second floor before more opposition showed. One man blazed away with a six-gun, but Ned cut him down with two .45 rounds. They charged down the first floor. Rebecca had pulled the eight-stick bomb from her shoulder bag and pushed in a one-foot fuse. She wedged the dynamite beside the main inside wall and lit the fuse.

They headed out the back door. Only one man showed, and he held both hands high over his head.

212

Outside they saw they were near the stables. Two men fired at them with revolvers, and Ned returned fire with both barrels of his shotgun. The riflemen rushed away behind the stables.

Rebecca and Ned reloaded their shotguns as they ran toward the horse barn.

"The Buzzard will try to make a run for it on a horse," Rebecca said. "He's a small man, not much over five feet tall, and slender."

In the darkness they had trouble telling who was who. Two horses pranced around where they had been saddled just outside the livery. Another horse blasted from the darkness of the barn and nearly ran them down, making them jolt to the side and allowing no time to draw and fire. The rider charged toward the open gate and quickly out of range as he headed north toward the mountains.

"That was him," Rebecca said.

Just then the bomb in the house went off. Every window in the place shattered outward. The main structure sagged; then the front porch caved in, and gradually the third floor gently collapsed until it became the first floor.

They watched a moment in fascination, then two handguns fired at them from the side of the barn. They returned fire with their own revolvers.

"Those two mounts, we can use them to chase him," Rebecca said. They grabbed the two horses meant for two of the Buzzard's guards, and wheeled after him. Rebecca lighted one more of the grenades and threw it behind the horse barn as they left. It went off with a roar and was followed by a series of screams of the wounded bandits.

Just outside the gate, Rebecca cautioned Ned, and they both stopped. She listened. Her ears, long trained as an Oglala, picked up the beat of the horse's hooves. She turned to the north.

"We can track him by sound as long as he keeps

moving," she said. They rode north for a quarter of a mile. They were well out of the town now, to the east of the pueblo, and nearing the foothills with their growth of pine.

They stopped again. This time she could hear nothing. They waited five minutes; then Rebecca nodded.

"He's started walking his mount. Now he's swinging around to the west, probably trying to get back to town."

They rode hard that direction for five minutes, then stopped and listened again. Ned couldn't hear a thing except some night birds and chirping crickets.

Rebecca smiled in the moonlight. "He's close by, and not moving. We wait him out. It shouldn't take long. *El Zopilote* is not a patient man."

CHAPTER 21

This time they had to wait ten minutes for the crafty Mexican bandit to move. When he did, it was with a rush. His horse took off across the dark landscape at a gallop.

Rebecca and Ned followed him at a slightly slower pace. They stopped each three or four minutes to check on his direction. Now it seemed that he was heading back for town. There he would try to find some help or to hide.

"Can we cut him off?" Ned asked as they rode faster than they normally would at night through the sparse vegetation of the open country.

"I'm not sure," Rebecca said. "If we tried to get around him, he might head the other way, and we can't split up. Then I'd have more than one sound to hear."

They stopped again, and she frowned. "There are more than a dozen horses out there in front of us, not just *el Zopilote*."

Before Ned could respond, they heard a half dozen pistol and rifle shots. Then all was still.

"The hoof beats are silent," Rebecca said. "I'm not sure what's happening."

They listened again, and gradually she began to smile. "He's heading back this way, and ten or twelve horses seem to be herding him."

"That I don't understand," Ned said. "Maybe he met ten of his mounted men, and they're now chasing us."

"Can't be. Why then the shots, and his sudden stopping? No, I think someone else out there knows that the Buzzard is trying to break out of the area. We have him between the two of us."

They walked their horses toward the sound of the oncoming mounts. Once they stopped to listen again, and Rebecca frowned in the moonlight. They could see only twenty or thirty feet ahead.

"I'm not sure what's happening. When I had just one sound, just one horse, it was easy. Now I get a whole jumble."

Ten minutes later they saw a line of horsemen walking toward them out of the dimness of the moonlight.

"Hello. Who are you?" Ned shouted.

"I am Hawk Caller" a voice came back.

"Come on in," Ned said, and the line continued. Soon Hawk Caller and nine other Pueblo Indians, all mounted and armed, walked their mounts up to the pair.

Five minutes later they had decided. The Buzzard had been between them, but in the confusion he had slipped out. The good part was that there was only one way that he could have gone.

"We have ten men across the approaches to Taos from here," Hawk Caller said. "He can't go that way. If he does, we will get two pistol shots as a warning."

"Which means he's on a long ride south, all the way to Santa Fe," Rebecca said with a sigh. "How can I track him in the dark."

Hawk Caller smiled and held out two kerosine lanterns.

"Not even an Oglala can track in the dark, but with white-eye light she can."

Rebecca shook one of the lanterns and pushed it back and forth. It was full of kerosine. At once she kicked her horse into motion toward the south road to Santa Fe, with Ned close at her heels.

It took her almost an hour to find his prints. The other hoofprints on the roadway had been crossed and recrossed by a host of nightime bugs and worms and a snake or two, all leaving their trails over the prints.

She found one line of hoof marks that had no bugs or worm tracks on them. New, less than an hour old.

"Has to be the Buzzard," she said. Rebecca looked at Ned. "You don't have to come along."

"Try and stop me."

Four of the Taos Pueblo Indians had been designated as long-range hunters. They had rolls of food across their backs and more ammunition than the others. Hawk Caller stayed as well, and the other Pueblos went back to help screen the town against the Buzzard's return.

The party of seven headed down the trail. They galloped for a quarter of a mile, then lit the lanterns and checked to be sure that the Buzzard's tracks were still on the roadway. The Pueblos were excellent trackers.

They did the quarter-mile jump three times and found the fresh horse prints each time. The system worked well, and they figured they were narrowing the gap between them and the hard-riding *el Zopilote*.

"He's still galloping that animal too much," Rebecca said, looking at the puffs of dust thrown up off the hoof tracks. "If he keeps this up for another hour, the horse will go down on him."

They slowed their pace between checks. Six more times they found tracks, but on the seventh, the prints were gone. They had just come through a small canyon and now began to backtrack to see how far the

217

prints would show on the road.

Quickly they discovered that their own mounts' prints had washed out those of the bandit. They sat there for a moment; then Rebecca lit the second lantern and gave it to one of the Indians. Hawk Caller looked at her.

"Tell him to take the far side of the wagon road and work back along it until we find fresh horse prints where the Buzzard left the road. We don't know which side he turned off. Then we'll track him again."

This was a one-person job, and Rebecca took one ditch and the Indian the other. They worked along two hundred yards before the Indian let out a cry, and everyone ran his way. The prints were plain coming away from the road.

Rebecca went ahead, following the hoof marks on foot. She noticed they were closer together. The animal was walking. A little farther on over the dry landscape she found where the horse was dragging one foot.

Fifty feet ahead, near the small stream that came down from Taos, they found the horse, down and pawing at the ground.

"Now the tracking really begins," Rebecca said. She took out one of her .44's and put the downed horse out of its misery, then swung the lantern around until she found the footprints. The Mexican wore cowboy boots with a square heel that left a sharp impression in the dirt.

For a mile the tracks followed the river south. *El Zopilote* could use it as a direction, and get water whenever he needed it. He seemed to be making good time, with a firm stride, but not a very long one. Then she remembered he was a small man.

How long he would last depended on how much stamina he had. She had sent the horses on ahead down the road. They were each to ride a mile beyond

218

the next man and wait and watch. Five of them would stretch out five miles from where they started. When the first horseman on the road saw her coming with the lantern, he was to move on ahead past the next rider five miles down the road.

Rebecca didn't think the Buzzard could last that long. He had been living a luxurious life these last two years. He was small and a little heavy and out of shape. She would find him within three miles.

She could soon tell that he knew they were tracking him. He veered away from the road so he couldn't see it, but kept to the southern course. Twice he circled back and crossed his trail and walked the same steps, but it was child's play for a talented tracker like White Squaw.

The trail led on. It was taking longer than she had guessed. She had heard the horses moving by on the road. No need for them yet.

Later she saw the sky lighten in the east, and soon she blew out the lantern. At least they had another part of the plan. Now those along the road would move out on this side and form a net across the route south and slowly ride north trapping the bandit chief somewhere between them and her.

El Zopilote would stumble into the line of horsemen before he knew they were there.

A small feeder stream came from the left and cut across the trail. Sitting on the far side of the foot-deep creek was *el Zopilote*, bathing his face with a wet cloth. He looked up and smiled.

"Well, you took long enough getting here," he said in perfect English. "What have you been waiting for?"

She walked closer. He didn't seem to be armed. What was his trick?

"I thought you'd give out long before now," Rebecca said.

"When a man runs for his life, he runs hard."

219

"It isn't how hard a man runs; it is what he is running from."

"Yes, the lady is right. I misjudged you. How could you do it so easily? In only a few days you bludgeoned and shot up and dynamited everything it took me twenty years to build up."

"Sometimes the gods smile on those in the right."

His hands were in his lap now, and he seemed to sway for a moment; then he steadied. He sat there cross-legged, watching her.

"You are a strange one to speak of the gods, White Squaw. Oh, I have heard of you. You must have killed my friend the skull-man, did you not?"

"Yes. He was a cold-blooded murderer. He got what he deserved."

"It would seem that is the rule of the day. But what of you, White Squaw? What do you deserve?"

"I received my punishment for my misdeeds long before I had a chance to do any. I have still not caught up to put the scales in balance."

"The town tamer is with you?"

"On the road. Are you ready to come back and face your trial in the *gringo* court?"

"Soon. Soon I will be ready. Come refresh yourself at the stream. Wash your pretty face, bathe if you wish. Then I will be ready."

"No tricks, I can call in six good men to help me."

"No tricks. The time of tricks is over."

He swayed again, but caught himself. She moved closer. His face seemed pale. But she knew he had been on a torturous walk most of the night. He was tired. At least he would have time to rest before he was hung.

She watched him carefully as she went to the water upstream from him. Rebecca did wash her face and her arms, then drank from the cool, pure mountain water and watched the Buzzard again.

He swayed and fell to the left, but pushed himself up.

"I . . . I am all right, just a little light-headed from the long run. Soon now we can start back for the village."

"It is no longer your village. You no longer have control over the men or families of the Mexicans in Taos."

His eyes closed, and his head sagged for a moment before he blinked and sat up straight.

"Are you ill?" she asked. "Your color seems to be pale. I'll call the men to come bring a horse."

"Don't be kind, woman!" he snarled at her. "Not at this point. I spit on your kindness!" It seemed to take most of the strength he had left. He looked at her, his eyes pleading, then he fell to the side and didn't stir.

She moved up cautiously, one of the .44's in her hand. He would have more tricks, she was sure.

She smelled it before she saw it. Her Indian nose caught the sweet unforgettable odor of blood. She ran the last few steps to him. He lay on his side, his hands where they had been by his legs. He had been sitting cross-legged so that she couldn't see his hands.

Now she could. Both wrists had been cut deeply. His legs and boots were covered with his blood. He had sat there and talked with her, then scolded her, and all the while he was bleeding to death. She checked his eyes. They were open. She closed the lids, and they stayed closed. She pinched his nose. There was no attempt to breathe through his mouth.

Antonio Sinfuegos, *el Zopilote*, was dead.

She fired two shots into the air, and soon two horsemen came riding up. One was Ned Silver and the other Hawk Caller. Ned looked down at the body and shook his head.

"I never thought he'd end it this way."

221

"He was tired; he must have decided the final result would be the same however it happened. This way he could decide the time and the method. That's a choice most men and women never get to make for themselves."

Life had returned to normal in Taos.

The Pueblo Indians had decided that they had satisfied their revenge for the deaths of their three guards at the sacred cave by the final end of *el Zopilote*. They had known of Rebecca's war preparations and watched her on her way to Sinfuegos' fortress.

When Ned Silver had come, they had sent him on her trail and then mounted ten warriors to follow and stand by to be of any assistance they could be. Ten more had followed to guard the entrance to the town. Now the blood debt had been paid. They were satisfied.

The treasures of their ancestors were safe. Already a team of workmen had gone to the cave to begin a new pueblo there. It would house only a small number of people and would be primarily for the protection of the cave. The gods and the spirits of their ancestors were pleased.

Rebecca had thanked Gray Squirrel and the people of the pueblo for their hospitality and moved back to the hotel.

June demanded that Rebecca come to her cafe every day for three square meals, and they talked and gossiped and plotted over every one.

Ned Silver had relaxed his insistence on the strict enforcement of the old laws. The city council had voted out the saloon closing law, but decided to keep the gun law in effect. Times were changing. What did a man need a gun for in town? It would hold down on the shootings and killings, and help them

222

keep the wild teamsters in line.

The council voted to look over the other old laws on the books and bring any up to date that needed it and vote to repeal any that were no longer useful. The citizens had started coming to every meeting of the council, and there was a growing interest in what they did and how they did it.

A lively contest had built already for the election of a new sheriff.

Josh Randall set up a special vote of the council to award Ned Silver an extra hundred dollars for a job well done. The next day Josh resigned from the council citing pressing business duties as the reason.

Ned bowed out of his thirty-day contract. He tore up the document himself. He and Rebecca took the four hundred dollars the city council paid him and put it in the Taos State Bank in the name of the Taos Pueblo, with Hawk Caller as the signature needed to withdraw the money. They explained to Hawk Caller that the money was to help the Pueblos when nothing else would work. They might need some new saws or axes to help build the new pueblo at the cave. Hawk Caller was to tell Gray Squirrel but no one else about the money and where it came from.

That evening in Rebecca's hotel room, she watched Ned sit up in bed and marveled again at his broad shoulders and muscled back. Naked men were beautiful.

"You haven't answered my question yet," he said, turning and kissing her breasts.

"Ask me again."

"Rebecca Caldwell. Would you do me the honor of spending a week or two with me in Denver, as my guest, for a lavish tour of the city, and a luxurious stay in the best hotel suite in town?"

"Well . . . you would be my guide around this spiffy town of Denver?"

"Of course."

223

"Would you be my personal live-in guest in my suite at this lavish hotel?"

"Absolutely. Try to keep me out."

She sat up, her pert, still-scarlet breasts bouncing as she kissed him.

"Yes, I think I'd like to spend some time in Denver. It's not far out of my way. I'm really heading to Texas to see my stepson, Joe Ridgeway. But that can wait a week or two."

"Or three, or more?" Ned suggested.

She frowned. "You just gave away four hundred dollars, more than a working man's pay for a year. Are you a working man? How do you plan to finance this luxurious vacation for us in Denver now that you're without funds?"

Ned chuckled, then bent and kissed her and pushed her slowly back on the bed. "I'll figure out a way, never fear. Right now I want to figure you out. We've got all night, until the stage leaves in the morning for Santa Fe."

Rebecca smiled. Tonight, in her bed, she would help him figure out about anything he wanted to. It was going to be a tremendously fine two weeks!